April 10, 2018

For Jill and Stephen – the best neighbors anyone could wish for – lovely, intelligent snowbirds who are flying back north again to their second home in New Hampshire, a home not far from Lake Winnepausaukee where my son went to summer camp. That was in 1975 – or more 45 years ago...

With fondest regards, Marilu

The cross-eyed god

by

Ursula Wilfriede Schneider

FIRST EDITION

UNIVERSITY EDITIONS, Inc.
59 Oak Lane, Spring Valley
Huntington, West Virginia 25704

Cover by Mark Grosskopf

Dedication

For Helge and for Elizabeth without whose generous and warm-hearted assistance this book could not have been published.

Table of Contents

I

Mentwab
(The Beautiful)

Off and on through the dark the bachelor heard the cricket sing. His night was filled with dreams that constantly woke him. Opening his eyes, still semi asleep, he cocked his ear toward the gaping window and listened to the cricket. It sang so softly he could hardly hear it. He strained his eyes trying to penetrate the dark foliage beyond the thin, white curtain even though he knew his sense of sight could not help him. The night was without a moon. It was dark. Sometimes the cricket stopped altogether. It seemed to him then as if his heart too had ceased to beat. Fear like a fiery spring rose from his chest. Its hot waters burned his throat and contracted his nostrils. For seconds he was unable to breathe and his hands gripped the sheets of his bed until he felt sweat between his clammy fingers. Lying on his back he strained every muscle in his body as if by sheer will power he could turn himself into one huge ear. When he heard the cricket again, he relaxed. His body became limp as if inundated in a brook. Closing his eyes, he suddenly saw Orphelia after she was found drowned carrying a large wreath of flowers and moss in her hair. He thought he could smell their faint odor. Tears, without him noticing it, trickled slowly down his temples. They got lost in the thickness of his hair.

It was mid October. Autumn with its splendid colors had arrived. The crickets had sung in great abundance all summer long. They had immersed his solitary nights with sounds that meant more to him than those of the greatest musicians. The insects were about to die. There was nothing he could do to prevent it. It had happened at the end of each summer as long as he could remember.

He thought how strange it was that as he grew older his memory became clearer as far as his early childhood was concerned. When it came to the present, it was the reverse. He sometimes forgot important events or even simple things like doctors' appointments. Worst of all, he could not recall where he put the street address or phone number of his dentist. His remembrance abandoned him slowly. It dropped like brown leaves off a majestic tree.

American and European childhoods were not so different from his own in East Africa where he was raised until his sixth year. It was in Ethiopia where his Armenian father and German mother had met by accident. It had not been a happy union. One marriage partner was part of the 20th century of Western standards. The other shared Eastern and Oriental beliefs that had more in common with the late 18th century moral system.

The bachelor's father belonged to the time of James Bruce. In 1770 the Scottish explorer had discovered the source of the Blue Nile hidden for so long in the shallow, brown waters of Lake Tana, set high above sea level, southwest of the Simien Mountains. Before Bruce had followed the Blue Nile and had seen its almost unapproachable, mist shrouded falls from a village called Tissisat, meaning *water that smokes*, he had gone inland on another long, terrible journey from Massava at the Red Sea to Gondar. Once Gondar had been the capital of Ethiopia. It had risen to fame with the reign of Emperor Fasiladas in 1632 and lasted until the fall of Tewodros in the latter part of the 19th century. During a time span of over two hundred years a dozen castles were built by various rulers. The palaces are a mixture of Moorish and European designs but their most intriguing designs follow the tradition of Axum, Ethiopia's most ancient city.

Not far from Gondar stood the now ruined castle of Kusquam. It was here where Bruce met Mentwab, the beautiful Ethiopian queen when she was old and told him

6

many stories about her life. The one Bruce liked best concerned her son. For many years the queen had managed to hide the death of her husband whom she had loved and, like Herzeloide, the mother of Parzival, had raised her son on her own. She wanted to make sure that her only child, once grown, would become king.

It did not help either, that the bachelor's parents, especially his mother, had been too young and inexperienced on their wedding day. They knew little about life, less about themselves, and nothing about each other as representatives of two totally different civilizations. They were not able to overcome their severe cultural collision.

Sometimes his parents' relationship reminded him of Lake Shala hidden among the Ethiopian mountains. The serene surface of the water had torn his heart. He had become the lone pelican that floated in front of the horizon on top of the glittering lake. Each time a swimmer enters the lake, he is embraced within a hundred silky folds. Yet every fish that the rivers carry into it, dies. They cannot live in potassium. Lake Shala and its rivers are unable to merge without causing death.

The bachelor's father was a practical man who was born with a large dose of common sense. This character trait was supported by his entire family. As in most old Armenian households, his preferred status as a male and as the only son was made clear to him at an early age. He had his mother's unwavering affection and was secure in his father's pride.

There had been an older brother born in Addis Ababa. He was the handsome and healthy heir who had been adored by his mother and father alike. Their two daughters counted far less. At the age of twelve, the older brother had an attack of tonsillitis. After the successful removal of his tonsils, the boy rode home from the hospital on the back of a mule. A man servant held him firmly in his lap. Either the long mule ride on a dusty road or inadequate antibiotics in Ethiopia, a country that knew little about modern medicine, caused an infection. The boy was dead within a few days.

A Coptic priest sang mass. He joined the orthodox Armenian cleric in charge of funeral services. He was dressed in a long, flowing robe whose borders were heavily

7

embroidered with gold threads. A large, black hood hid half his face and black beard. His outfit frightened small children. They screamed at the top of their lungs when he tried to reach out to them.

Paid wailing women, their bare feet leaving imprints of toes and heels on the dirt road, lamented behind the coffin while it was carried four miles from the dead boy's home to the churchyard. The women tore at their hair and their dirt encrusted fingernails clawed faces and breasts. Beneath their professional tears, they watched as large rocks were heaved upon the grave so at night—with the boy left in his tight, airless grave—the hyenas could not unearth the child's body and feast upon it. The churchyard lay quietly in a dazzling sun. Long after everyone had left, the sobs of the boy's mother still seemed to fill the air. Her crying had accompanied every shriek of the wailers throughout the funeral ceremonies.

The bachelor's Armenian grandparents were hard-working, intelligent people. They had escaped the cruel Turkish exodus in 1918, which forced them from their land and home upon the Black Sea. Separately, they came to Ethiopia where hope rested in their son's ability to bring them in touch with the blessings of modern times. They lived as though still in the 18th century, and were unable to move forward without their son's help. Their son, together with his wife, was not only expected to bestow upon them a grandson, but to also provide them with a laundry room, and with hot water in their kitchen.

When their son married a German rather than the wealthy Armenian girl who for several years had been his family's choice, the bachelor's Armenian grandmother cried. She foresaw great unhappiness.

* * *

Reclining sleeplessly on his back and his eyes wide open, the bachelor saw himself as a four-year-old child surrounded by his Armenian grandmother and about ten elderly ladies who had come for their regular mid-week afternoon visit.

* * *

8

His grandmother rested under a large, winged mirror that controlled the living room. It was suspended above an old-fashioned, spacious sofa and whoever sat under it was reflected in all four corners of the room. His grandmother's figure was omnipresent. She could be seen at once by everyone in the farthest end of the room. The seat under the mirror was the seat of honor. It was the center of the household from where orders were given to white-dressed, bare-footed servants and younger members of the family.

His grandmother's gray hair was parted in the middle and tied severely at the neck. He had never seen it undone. Her hair contrasted with the black dress she wore with simple dignity. She spoke four languages fluently, among them Turkish and Amharic—but could neither read nor write. Her cooking skills were superb, and when it came to embroidery, she was close to being an artist. Her needle work belonged to a much older tradition than the one of Venetian lace-makers. She suffered from diabetes, was obese and unusually tall. She lived a sad life steeped in superstition and boredom. Since she was bright but could not read, she depended upon the oral instruction she received from a taciturn, much older husband and from Armenian women of all ages with little or no formal education.

Every Wednesday afternoon his grandmother's living room contained several stately ladies whose short, stout figures were dressed in black. Relatives or close neighbors constituted the majority of these. His grandmother's youngest, dark-haired daughter, silently assisted by a thin Ethiopian maid, served delicious coffee in fragile demitasse cups. The strong Turkish coffee was always accompanied by a freshly baked Armenian delicacy. Food and drinks were prepared in a kitchen that resembled a shack during the years of the gold rush in the United States. There were no windows. Here and there the walls had big openings through which one could see the neighbors' kitchens. They were in no better state. There was a wood stove and water had to be stored in large containers. Every pail had to be carried up a steep flight of stairs. During the rainy season, torrents of water gushed through parts of the wall and inundated a warped floor. There was hardly a spot on the ceiling that remained dry.

9

Everything was damp and dark. The kitchen also served as a place where the weekly bath was taken.

On Saturday nights a tub was put in the middle of the kitchen and filled with warm water. Then the bachelor's grandmother scrubbed vigorously her grown son's broad back. Every so often, when she saw red scratches on his shoulders, she asked him where they had come from. He did not tell her that they were love tokens from the women with whom he had slept.

The old women, who met on Wednesday afternoons, their hands busily engaged with intricate needlework, talked about domestic chores, marriages, deaths, and births. The expected arrival of a newborn baby was a major event. For weeks, especially in the beginning of a pregnancy and toward the end of it, the women gossiped endlessly about the health of mother and child.

Whenever possible, a room was put up for the anticipated infant. Its first toys and jewelry, usually a golden wrist band with the name of the baby engraved in it or a cross to be worn around a tiny, wrinkled neck were prepared with sharp attention to details. So were the infant's clothes and minute, wooden bed that was painstakingly painted. The embroidery on small bed sheets and matching pillow cases took months to accomplish. It was outstanding workmanship and designed to last for several generations. The colors were the traditional blue for boy, and pink for girl, with some yellow as a neutral hue. Several months before the baby's birth its room was proudly shown to guests. In case of a first pregnancy, the furniture, carpet and sometimes even curtains glowed in blue. It became the blue room. Beyond its windows often long branches of Eucalyptus trees, the landmark of Addis Ababa, swayed gently. If a girl was born instead, the Armenians, especially the male members of the family, did not hide their disappointment. Even at birth women were treated as second class citizens.

It was quite easy to foretell the gender of the unborn child. As soon as the stomach protruded a little, which sometimes did not occur until six months after conception, especially with a first baby, the expectant mother was asked to slowly walk up and down in front of an experienced, old woman. If the silhouette of the mother-to-be, when viewed

10

from the back, did not reveal her state, she carried a boy. Boys stood out in front only. Girl's also changed somehow the mother's anatomy in the back. Her hips were thought to be suddenly wider and her elongated back protruded more. The cause of heartburn was also explained in a special way. If the pregnant woman during her last two months suffered from a burning discomfort behind the lower part of the sternum or from another kind of indigestion, accomplished Armenian women firmly believed the heartburn occurred because the fetus grew hair. Had these simple women been told that the aches of the expectant mother were caused by the loss of space of the esophagus and abdominal regions because of the embryo's growth, they would not have believed it.

After the baby's birth immediate rites were performed. A small golden cross was attached to the blue, painted head of the bed. A pin containing a blue stone was fastened to his waddling clothes above his chest. The blue stone encased in gold prevented the evil eye. Certain Armenians were accused of possessing this ability to cause evil. Especially if they were withered widows, slightly hunchbacked from age—the ones who were no longer able to defend themselves.

* * *

Many years had passed since then. In a house built at the foot of the Watchung mountains twelve miles west from New York, the bachelor tossed open-eyed among sheets that had become entangled with his body. Crumbling and hot they clung to his limbs. As soon as he closed his eyes, one picture after another rose in front of him. One in particular absorbed his attention. He saw his mother as the young, beautiful woman she had once been.

Unable to sleep, he recalled her having told him that when he was only about three weeks old, he had been exposed to a long row of visiting ladies during an afternoon at his grandmother's house in Addis Ababa. They had made a great fuss about him. They had fondled him and spoken to him in those special baby sounds which, like music, effortlessly cross all linguistic borders since they belong to a realm where no words are necessary. Meaning is conveyed in a sublingual form. But, all this adoration had exhausted mother and child.

The infant, after the departure of his visitors, whimpered for what seemed like hours. His unhappiness could not be overcome by food or a change of diapers. Even the cloth tying his tiny legs from thigh to Achilles tendon so that they, according to Armenian belief, would not be bowed, had been removed. Now, too tired to sleep, the child lay on his grandmother's wide, white bed whose springs allowed a rocking motion that usually put him to rest quite quickly.

That afternoon nothing worked. All the French, English, and German nursery rhymes had been sung. They were only interrupted by the softest cooing that poured forth from his grandmother's lips. Those Armenian sounds fluttered like caged doves above the infant's head. They were the only ones his mother liked in this tongue that otherwise sounded ugly to her. These words were incantations, mystic prayers whose wisdom and goodness had endured the most difficult test of all: time.

His grandmother's arms ached from rocking her huge bed. Suddenly, she lifted her large body into an upright position and walked out of the darkened bedroom. When she returned, she held a porcelain saucer with cotton wool on it. She quickly placed both on the baby's chest. Before the mother knew what was happening, the grandmother had set the cotton wool on fire. The child, whose eyes had been semi-closed opened widely in a catlike manner. Then his little face distorted like that of a horrified old man. His snivel became a shriek, followed by loud cries that mingled with the mother's shrill sounds of protest. She was beside herself for she thought her baby's torso and face were going to be burned. Crying and clasping the infant in her arms, she hurdled at her speechless mother-in-law whatever insults she could muster in Italian—the language in which mother and grandmother communicated. The old Armenian lady had acted in good faith. Now she tried in vain to calm her daughter-in-law's rage. According to an ancient Armenian custom the flames of the cotton, blessed by the Armenian priest, counteracted the evil eye.

That night, back at her own home at the outskirts of Addis Ababa and not able to sleep, the boy's mother threw on her dressing gown. Quietly, she went into their walled-in compound that contained not only their own house but also a smaller one where the servants and their children slept. She walked back and forth on the gravel ground and woke up their night watch man, called Zabania. His tall, thin figure was wrapped in a white *shamma*, the national Ethiopian dress. He had fallen asleep over a small fire he had built to keep himself warm in the chilly mountain night.

Suddenly, as she moved silently in her small garden, she remembered the myth of Demeter's search for her daughter Kore, also known as Persephone. The young woman, ignoring the eyes of the Zabania who followed her steps through the semi-darkness, stopped moving about. She no longer heard the dogs issuing their nightly barks throughout the neighborhood. Instead she saw the Greek corn goddess, disguised as an old woman, putting Celeus' child in the fire. She remembered that night after night Demeter burned the infant's mortal nature away until she was interrupted by Metanira, wife of Celeus and queen of Eleusis. That way Demeter was hindered from making the child immortal as she had planned. But try as she might, the young woman was unable to picture her mother-in-law as Demeter. She was incapable of detecting even a fraction of the goddess' noble proportions in her mother-in-law's bulky body, as it slowly decayed under loose, black clothes.

In Greek fashion yet with Alexander the Great still unborn for more than three hundred years after Yerevan had been founded, Armenian custom still assigned women to take care of infants and toddlers. Until the boy was about four years old his father had little interest in him. Husbands and young fathers did not know how to handle their small offspring. At best they took them for a ride in their cars or drove them to a relative's home to show them off.

The boy's father was a passionate hunter. He was happiest when he could spend his weekends in Ethiopia's bush. The countryside within the vicinity of Addis Ababa was magnificent. High plateaus spanned numerous mountain tops like vast bridges. Flat space undulated imperceptibly like a calm sea and was covered with grass and trees. Like huge tabletops that had been split apart, the even stretches sometimes broke off without warning and disappeared into deep crevices. Once in a while a mountain was eroded to the extent that it resembled a huge column. Its phallic shape stood defiantly in empty space and challenged the sky.

Often tiny villages numbered just a few huts. Their round grass roofs had a hole in the middle to allow the smoke from cooking fires to escape. The walls of the circular sheds were made from twigs and cow dung. The huts huddled in the shade of a high, wooded hill whose crest was dominated by a herd of baboons. Under the opening of the huts, away from the fire in the middle of the dark interior, small children intermingled with emaciated goats and starving, flea and worm-infested dogs. Occasionally, a scrawny donkey or two could be seen as well. The large herds of cattle outside the village belonged to wealthy landowners. But most cows, adorned with great, wing-like horns and dreamy eyes, were so thin that each rib could be counted.

In some villages baboons outnumbered their inhabitants. Man and beast were constantly at war with each other. This was especially so at harvest time when the monkeys raided the meagerly growing grain, called Tef. It was used to make injera, a greenish-gray, flat, soft bread most poor Ethiopians live on. The villagers, dressed in rags, carried old rifles whenever affordable, or at least large knives and sticks when they walked through their territory. Barefoot, tall, thin-legged, with angular faces in which their dark eyes seemed to be made from patches of velvet and silk, they moved noiselessly among twigs and low hanging branches studded with thorns. They held their finely-shaped heads high. Moving lightly, they relied on their small ears and noses to tell them about invisible foes that lurked in the bushes.

The villagers, men, women and children alike, had a strong body odor. If one met them in a group, the smell of their unwashed bodies, dressed in rags, was intense. Just before harvest time one could see several men sitting all night on a wooden seat, eight to ten feet high, overlooking their small patches of land. For hours the men uttered at infrequent intervals a short, ferocious cry. Tirelessly, they beat sticks whose clatter prevented baboons and wild pigs to ravish the crops their lives depended upon.

The Ethiopians were usually glad to see a hunting party such as the boy's father frequently arranged for his friends. It interrupted their routine and they were eager to serve as guides. It was often their only means to earn a little extra money of which they were in great need. Their wives, with babies slung across their hips because their backs were burdened with heavy, earthen water jugs or huge bundles of fire wood, sat for hours as close as possible to the camp. They formed a colorful half-moon circle around the tents and vehicles. The women were always careful to keep their distance so they would not be chased away by the cook or the hired men who guarded the land-rovers and jeeps. In subdued voices they chatted with each other.

Each time a safari member came within the vicinity of this living enclosure, the women's faces lit up with hope, exposing flawless teeth. More than once they waited all day to get some morsels of food. Any empty can, regardless of its former content, was eagerly snatched up, later to be carried back to their village. Most babies and children's eyes were infested with flies that hung at the edges of their eyelids. No one bothered to chase them away. Among thick lashes the flies crawled brazenly from one corner of the eye to the other. They descended slowly to nose and mouth, lingered there for a while, then, without haste, walked back to the eyes, their favorite spot. Eye infections, some of them serious, were common. No medication or doctor was available for miles. A bottle of mouthwash with its disinfectant component was a miracle water competing with the one at Lourdes.

Approaching the villagers meant not only defying the flies, but also overcoming the awful stench that issued from their bodies. Though the Ethiopians knew what a bath was, none of them was able to take one. The water of rivers and lakes was cold. So was the air. Soap was a luxury no one could afford. It was always chilly, even at noon when the sun stood straight above. As the villagers, old ones mingling with babies, sat rolled up in heaps of clothes, they smelled so terribly, one could not approach them without disgust. Many times, only their bare feet with soles hard as torn leather, and heads with eyes whose allurement neither flies nor infections could diminish, were visible.

The boy's father was a skilled hunter who had received his first rifle while still a child. Broad-shouldered and small-waisted with legs somewhat short, so an almost perfectly proportioned body was not in balance, he could hunt for hours without showing any signs of fatigue. When his sharp eye spotted a prey, he pursued it mercilessly. Caught by hunting fever, he was able to run down ravines that could break a man's neck while climbing them cautiously.

Whether his father wore a khaki uniform while on safari, or a business suit, his walk at all times was executed with inwardly turned toes. It was exactly the opposite from the way his mother moved. When the boy started to grow up and reflected more upon the vast differences of his parents, he thought the manner they walked was one of the easiest ways to spot their most characteristic traits. To the boy the inward-turned toes of his father symbolized self-control.

Born with a sense for business, his father attended to daily tasks with considerable circumspection. He was content to move mostly within family, work and a few old friends. His loyalty toward his clan was sharp and narrow like a cliff where the sun never touches the bottom of the ravine. Yet his sense of duty did not reach beyond the immediate Armenian fate. He stood solidly in the midst of his family, comprised of three generations and cared little about the rest of the world. His practical mind and a hunter's eye saw beauty in almost every household item, including kitchen pots. The boy's father was content with reality. Even when young, he disliked exaggerations and suffered when his innate sense of symmetry was disturbed. Like Pan, the horned god of goats and wood nymphs, he loved the sun at noon and the stillness of uninhabited bush land and wild grass. Some of his father's finest gifts were Greek.

Looking closely there was a lot of the Roman in him too. A large amount of rather naively displayed cruelty went hand in hand with a drive for leadership and discipline. Though intelligent, he was not intellectually inclined. He did not try to understand matter, he used it. The universe was not there to be questioned or rationalized—it existed simply to live and act within. Any world permitting him the pleasure of good food, drink and sexual enjoyment, would serve him well. Sex was important. If not enough was made available within the bonds of marriage, it was sought elsewhere. He was wont to scorn male Ethiopians unless they had power and money, but he was less discriminating when he slept with their women.

16

The boy's mother was different. She hated reality. Even during moments of joy she was often ill-at-ease. By temperament and upbringing she was a romantic. Life was only desirable in the past or future. The present was like a drawer she had forgotten to close. Upon its sharp edges she cut the shin of her leg when she leaped off her chair. Living in her imagination, she could only bear reality after she had embroidered it in a rather illusive way. Always caught unaware by exaggeration, she felt she was either pulled heavenward or trampled upon by the hoof of a horse. Like a chicken in a stall she was not able to flee quickly enough from the kicking stallion. Sensitive to a point where the wrong color or sound could make her scream, it was not easy to live with her.

She loved her son and dreamt up the most elaborate future for him. Yet when it came to daily chores, she could quickly lose her temper and create an unpleasant atmosphere around herself. She surrounded herself with books she hoped would either become an impenetrable wall of fire or a void, whose iciness and sarcasm would defeat even the most ardent rescuer. Of course this never happened. She could not isolate herself from her surroundings. But nothing prevented her from reading. She read constantly. To become engaged in matters of the mind was an urgent need.

The boy's mother had the formal education his father did not, and both of his parents felt the reverse might have been better. His mother tried in vain to raise his father's aesthetic perception. But she discovered soon that she was only able to get him interested in an artistic level slightly above the old movies they saw in the generator-run cinemas of Addis Ababa. His father had been brought up in an environment where civilization was almost non-existent. Culture was an abstract concept for him. He was uneasy about it.

In the beginning of their marriage when the boy's father saw how important music and the arts were to his wife, he made an effort to understand the world in which she lived. After a short while though he lost interest. He was only three years older than his wife, yet in worldly ways far more mature than she. Daily decisions were briefly sorted out by him, then executed in an organized manner and a calm state of mind. Pop music and newspapers filled his inner void.

With the boy's mother life started slowly to go wrong. Since her marriage she avoided activity whenever possible, especially in the domestic sphere. Her days were confined to household chores where she obeyed day-in and day-out the same rules. Her unchanging routine was divided into compartments of children, husband, servants, pets and relatives. Her performance may have incarnated all the virtues desirable in a wife, but to her, marriage was close to a term spent in prison.

Her husband did not allow her to work or continue her education and she quickly lost most of her movement. Her house became her jail. She could only shift between her own household, her mother-in-law's and those of close relatives. Her former friends were subtly yet continuously discouraged from visits.

After three years, during which boredom and depression interchanged with temper tantrums, she was a different person. She had finally understood that her rage against the invisible chains with which her marriage had shackled her was useless. Sometimes at night when everyone else was asleep, she lay wide-eyed next to her slumbering husband or took a walk in their garden. At these times, she thought herself no longer human. She felt rather as if she had slid down the ladder of evolution, perhaps even taking a sideline, since she saw herself more and more like a rabbit or chicken who sat with ruffled feathers and broken bones in a corner. Yet however blurred her vision had become, somehow soon she saw again the wings of the horse who had just trampled her. Crouched in her corner, she dreamt of her white stallion breaking through the roof of its stall and flying into the night with her—chicken or not—perched on his back. She had given up God, but not Pegasus.

Even though still young and blood rushing strongly within good veins, the boy's mother was only partly alive. She felt caught by her unhappy marriage like a ship run aground. The sea that had carried her swiftly through high and dangerous waters no longer moved beneath her. Dead it lay beneath her feet. It was as if her heart had stopped beating. With burning eyes she sat in her living room and listened politely to her family and guests. Yet her mind was almost constantly somewhere else. Many times she was bored

18

to the point where her hands had to clutch a coffee cup, some needle work or a book in order not to scream. When boredom persisted too long, she became depressed. Nothing made sense any longer. She felt pushed to the ground where she turned into an albatross whose wings were being nailed to a piece of driftwood the sea had spit up.

At first the young woman did not know what she suffered from. She only noticed her immediate surroundings, house, husband, garden, servants, even her child, had lost their color. It was as if they had changed into pulpy, gray forms that moved about sluggishly and without aim. Everyone seemed to be asleep. Heads nodded as if overcome by great tiredness.

Her anxiety grew particularly strong during the four months of the rainy season in East Africa when storms poured buckets of water on their flat-roofed house. Like a river, the rain roared uninterruptedly for hours and turned shouts into whispers. Household members who sat so close to each other they could have touched hands, almost did not hear each other. The rain and dampness drowned their voices and immobilized their movements. Bound to their chairs, like Lorelei to her rock, everybody remained still. Toward the end of her third rainy season in Ethiopia, the world was as removed from her as if it had been put on the pedestal of a merry-go-round. Slowly, in a rather dignified and grotesque manner it moved to an inaudible tune. She watched it with wide, horrified eyes.

At night after the boy's mother had submitted to his father's amorous approaches, she lay quietly in the dark. She listened to the rain open-eyed, feeling how it pulled at every nerve of hers. Though exhausted, she did not dare to close her eyes. Sleep was a well whose slippery edges drew her sometimes by her feet first, sometimes by her head. Sleep was a garden snake trying to swallow a mouse. Aching for rest, she was terrified to be sucked into a bottomless darkness. If her feet were pulled first, she clung with all her strength to the edge of the well until she was unable to hold her weight any longer. Sleep, of course, always won. She was not able to wrestle all night like Jacob and his angel. Sometimes when she could not escape the horrible sense of falling, her muscles suddenly and powerfully, as if someone touched her with an electric rod, twitched in an involuntary movement. She then became aware how fast the black, slimy walls of the well rushed past her and she screamed.

As a child, while in a wooded summer camp perched like a nest on a mountain wall, she had dropped stones into an empty well that belonged to the ruins of an old castle. The three-hundred-year-old water hole had been built all the way down to the bottom of the mountain where it was met by a river. While listening to the drop of the stone, she counted. It always took a long time before she heard the stone hit the ground. Sometimes there was the faintest echo of a splash. Now, falling asleep, she had become this stone. From far she heard a voice counting as the rocky walls of the pit rushed past her with terrible speed. A rank, humid odor nauseated her. She felt like suffocating. No longer able to bear the falling sensation, she pulled her legs toward her stomach and howled. Afraid to wake her husband, she stifled her cry by stuffing the bed sheet into her mouth. Nevertheless, she sometimes woke him. Only half awake, he thought she had one of her nightmares.

* * *

Years passed swiftly. The boy's father was the first one to leave East Africa. He lived in New York for two years before the rest of his family joined him. The small boy's father wanted to continue the marriage. His mother did not even though the boy now had a little sister born a year and a half after his parent's wedlock. Their marriage had taken place after the boy's mother was seven months pregnant. She could hardly conceal her bulging stomach under the long, elaborate wedding gown that emphasized the waist. The boy was barely nine months old when his mother conceived again.

At first the boy's mother declined politely her husband's efforts to uphold the marriage. In her usual timid manner whose submissiveness most men, especially older ones, found irresistible she fought for a divorce. With more and more emotional emphasis, she kept saying no to her husband's persistence. She was deadly tired of their marriage and afraid of her husband. She did not know the back-breaking hardships that awaited her. With her lack of common sense

20

she had not considered practical things, such as a divorce and raising two children alone in a new, strange country where her prospects of finding a well paying job were limited. All she was intensely aware of was that she could no longer live with the man she married. She did not want her children to grow up in a family where husband and wife despised each other. She had seen what marital hate and fear did to children. She had been one of them.

The boy's aunt, his mother's only sister, had found them a pretty, somewhat dilapidated cottage in New Jersey. The young woman commuted back and forth to the city where she worked in a large office using her language skills. She did not know what lay in wait for her. But even if she had known, she would not have stayed with her husband. He knew she had serious doubts about their life together before she married him. Even after the birth of their second child she had attempted to break away. Her husband had hoped to reinforce their marriage with another child. But she felt as if he tried to tie the rope tighter around her neck.

One day when fear and desperation got the better of her, she took both their small children and went to Germany. For weeks she had made arrangements cladestinely and had taken only what she could carry. She was worried her husband might discover her plans to escape and prevent them from leaving East Africa. She had help from a small group of French teachers who gave her the psychological support she needed to get away. There was especially one young math teacher at the French Lycée of Addis Ababa whose carefree, laughing approach to life she adored. When she saw him, she felt as if she were looking at a mountain meadow in spring. Wherever she glanced, there were thousands of flowers dotted against the horizon. Nothing except light and sky. No child cried, no lunch needed to be prepared. No husband forced her to have sex with him.

She never got to know the teacher's face fully. He hid it under a soft, brown beard. For his sake she came to like most men with beards. To each beard she attributed some of the French instructor's qualities that had enticed her at a time when she was eaten alive by doubts, guilt and fear. She was young, had no self-esteem and did not know what life was all about.

21

Then one morning before she fully realized what was happening, the young woman and her children were airborne. The DC6-B, one of the few planes built strongly enough to take off and land in high altitudes, circled slowly above the Eucalyptus tree-studded city of Addis Ababa. She hoped she would never see this place again in which both of her children were born. Her husband, who was not without suspicion, had not been in time to head off her departure. Or perhaps he did not try hard enough to prevent her from leaving. Who knows, the young woman thought, as she peered with relief through the window of the ascending plane.

The boy's maternal grandparents had welcomed mother and children warmly in Germany. They tried to accommodate their daughter and grandchildren, both of whom still wore diapers. But when she attempted to find a job, it proved impossible to leave her one-and-a-half-year-old daughter and three-year-old son in her parent's charge. Her parents, divorced and remarried in both cases to younger spouses, could not be burdened with grandchildren. They still had their own lives to live that involved work and travel. After about three months and after her husband followed her to Germany, she reluctantly agreed to a reconciliation. Together husband, wife and the two small children returned to East Africa.

As the plane approached the landing strip which glowed embedded among Addis Ababa's noble mountains, her heart sank. Like someone drowning, a fast sequence of images unrolled the past three years of her marriage in front of her. While her husband held her hand, it was as if a black curtain descended rapidly, blinding her. With closed eyes, she pushed a prayer through her clenched teeth, hating herself for it. She considered herself an atheist. To pray in moments of extreme danger, imagined or real, was an act of cowardice. Loathing herself, as she crouched in her seat, she distinctly saw a mirror image of herself that had peeled off her like the skin of an onion. Her shadow slowly got up and retreated into the far end of the plane's cabin. For a moment she thought naively: "Death is not as horrible as I always imagined it to be."

The plane landed smoothly. Then, in the midst of her husband's undisguised pleasure to be home and their children's joyful excitement in spite of their long flight, there rose a scene in front of her eyes, she hoped she would never have to remember. While they had to go through tedious customs procedures and embraced some of her husband's Armenian relatives, an image she dreaded floated toward her. She thought she had locked this particular drawer of her memory tightly and thrown the key away. Yet somehow the receptacle sprang open.

Out of it came a small dining room, containing a table with several chairs. Against a wall stood a long, low hutch and in one corner of the room several clay flower pots were arranged in a colorful group. Suspended above the plants hung a couple of good etchings. The room had no windows. Had it not been for the more spacious living room that joined it without doors so only wooden beams separated one room from the other, the dining room would have not only lacked light but air as well.

It was after midnight and two people sat around the table. One of them was her fiancé, the other herself. After having known each other for almost two years, they had recently been through an extensive engagement ceremony. The event had been celebrated with considerable expense at the home of her husband-to-be. Her mother had flown in from Germany. Still slender and lovely, she sat among the somberly clad Armenian ladies, most of whom outweighed her mother by many pounds. An elderly Armenian priest, who wore a sumptuous black robe and a scarlet hood embroidered with pearls and semi-precious stones had—during a moment of solemn silence—betrothed the young couple. The hands of many family members and guests clapped their approval. From all corners of the room good wishes were conveyed with drinks and toasts. There were jokes and laughter during the rest of the night.

Her fiancé's mother was larger and more imposing than her husband, whose silver hairline reached only as far as the ear lobes of his wife. Through most of the evening the old woman never left her seat of honor under the mirror from where she oversaw that everyone had enough to eat and drink. As she enjoyed looking at the dancers, her tongue time and again wetted her lips and pushed her false front teeth in and out of their gums. Proudly, her eyes clung to her son's

23

handsome figure as he moved with an earthy grace to the music.

Later when her fiancé dropped her mother and herself off at her own place, he asked her to stay a few minutes in the car with him. She agreed but was little prepared for the violent assault her fiancé made in the name of love.

"Now you are mine," he kept saying as if he had just purchased her at a market. He pushed her into the corner of her seat and against the car door. Then he held her so firmly, she could hardly move and took full possession of her in a rough, ugly and painful way. Deliberately, he did not use any precaution. He wanted her to conceive.

"My father is old. He wants a grandson. I am his only son." He justified his onslaught.

As she watched the windows of the car getting foggy from their breath, she was not sure if she should laugh or cry. While she worried about her dress getting spotted and torn and her mother waiting for her inside the house who would ask questions about her disheveled appearance, it was all over.

This was the first instance her husband had penetrated her if she discounted the time in the beginning of their relationship when he had forced her to the bathroom floor of a roomy bungalow she shared with four other young women. Only when her fierce cries of protests alerted one of her roommates, did he cease his attempts to rape her. After that he did not touch her again until the day they pledged to marry.

The dining room scene occurred about five months after the eve of their engagement. The would-be bride was pregnant. The past weeks had painted her future life in no uncertain colors. She now knew what to expect as the wife of an ambitious and sexually overzealous Armenian in an isolated East African city. She did not like what she saw. The strange hues and shades frightened her. In her gullible way she had just finished expressing those fears openly toward her fiancé. She had spoken like a child who needed to be reassured in the dark. Great was her surprise when, instead of the hoped for consolation, her fiancé calmly put a gun on the dining room table and said with no visible emotion even though his face had turned white: "If you break our

24

engagement, I will kill you and me."

It was utterly ludicrous. She saw the two of them as the protagonists of a third-rate novel. In her confused state of mind she also imagined shot-gun marriages and most of all she visualized the Mayerling affair with Rudolf and poor Mary Vetsara dead in bed. She remembered her mother telling her that on January 30, 1889, the crown prince of Austria and his mistress had committed suicide rather than be married to someone else. Where she should have laughed, she took her fiancé's words seriously and cried helplessly.

Afterwards the boy's mother considered an abortion for weeks. But she did want a child. Not just a child by any man, but this Armenian's child. She did not know why. It does not make any sense, she thought unhappily, caught in a riddle she could not solve.

Already unsure if she was in love with him, and too inexperienced to understand what children were about, the young woman was idealistically inclined. Where she should have used common sense, she saw Madonnas in rose gardens whose beauty was enhanced by carrying a pudgy baby on their laps. The husband of a Madonna was rarely visible.

She was also pushed by biological facts that had given her a healthy, attractive body. To have a child seemed to be a natural undertaking. On a subconscious level, she still adhered to a four-thousand-year-old law. This law focused rather primitively, and if not obscenely then quite insultingly, on a woman's sexual organs. She was born for one purpose— to reproduce. There was no doubt she wanted a child, but not necessarily within the confinements of wedlock, nor because of an obsolete law.

The boy's father was, contrary to his mother, an experienced lover. He had enticed many women from different racial backgrounds during his passionate adolescence and was ready to settle down. Marriage altered his life little when compared with the drastic changes the boy's mother had to undergo. Of course, she could always imagine their marriage had saved three lives and her fiancé's pride. He felt a broken engagement would make him the laughing stock of the Armenian community in Addis Ababa in which he enjoyed the status of a privileged member. He was keen in keeping this distinction. For these reasons the marriage did take place and everybody lived happily for about three weeks afterward.

II

As the full-fed hound . . .
(Shakespeare)

The Statue of Liberty in New York, brainchild of a
French ambassador and the gift of thousands of French
school children who had helped to turn the ambassador's
dream into reality by contributing a penny a child to the
statue, had raised her arm to the boy's separately arriving
father and mother the same way she greeted every new
immigrant: Her pulchritudinous face was but stony
indifference. The boy's mother, at first a little intimidated by
this gargantuan symbol of the New World, later came to
admire it as a perfect metaphor of fate.

"Here I am," the statue spoke to her, "made of stone and
steel, and blind. I am hollow inside so you can climb-up
within me. If you get to my head, you will know why the
Greeks worshiped Pallas Athene, not only as the embodiment
of wisdom, but also as the ideal symbiosis of man and
woman."

The boy's mother, who never set foot inside the statue,
got to like it. She understood that its hollowness was an
optical illusion. In reality, the statue contained many levels.
Like Schliemann, one had to go seven layers deep, each time
thinking that the level reached was Troy, before one
discovered the actual one. Each stratum, like a translucent,
deep sea, embraced a new wave of immigrants.

First there were the proud British. Some of them
remembered, with the haunting persistence of the exiled,

ducal palaces where white deer had grazed on several acres of a carefully kept and fenced-in park.

There were the Irish who escaped the Potato famine. Their souls hungered forever for their green slopes high above a white, foaming sea. Scanning the sky, they saw *The Wild Swans at Coole*. They longed for the brown earth of Ireland rolling gently under a misty sky. At night they dreamt about a place where the ground was interrupted by mounds whose ancient bones and skulls kept their secret.

Then came the German farmers. They were the second and third sons, pushed out of their home by the first born who alone inherited the farm. Even after years of work that broke their backs and when they had arrived at a social status superior to that of their eldest brother who owned the soil in the old country, they still told their children and grandchildren about the snow-covered mountains they had left behind. During high holidays they talked about the black forests where a small deer had stood in the undergrowth and looked at them with luminous eyes, wide with fear. And without going to church their children learned about *Hymns to the Night*.

There were the Italians, their memories delirious from a sharp, white sun. Their sun is reflected upon dry land and the green-blue water of the shallow Mediterranean whose polluted beauty is fathomless. In their blood they carried the rocky parts of the sea. And they never forgot the purple grottoes south of Rome that hold sunken images of Tiberius and Caligula.

One could not overlook the French. They did not hesitate to let everyone know they were still *La Grande Nation* even though in their *City of Light*, no Sun king had ruled for over three hundred years. If the Italians had music in their throats and sang about a past glory no other country had produced in such eye-blinding fashion, the French still talked in the most civilized tongue of the world. They were forever in love with their educated women whose sounds add subtle seduction to a bland day.

The Greeks came too. Their shabby stores on Eighth Avenue and 42nd Street reveal nothing of Crete's ancient splendor, of Alexander the Great, master of the then known world. Sadly, they sing about his early death when he left the earth to his small son Kassandros, whose shoulders were not strong enough to hold it.

The icon carrying Russians also arrived. They were preceded by their bearded, literary giants who rode behind three horses across snow covered lands. Their borderless steppes burned the eyes with fire and encased their soul in iron chains. Their love was so desperate it could only end on the tracks of an oncoming train or in the icy waters of the Volga where *Lady Macbeth of Mtsensk* drowned clutching her rival.

Quite early the Jews entered. They still remembered the day when they had walked on the sandy bottom of the Red Sea and when Moses, his face swollen from anger and suffering, had turned Egypt into a land of darkness where sticks became hissing snakes.

She saw the Japanese too, the fine skinned women who tripped on their wooden platform shoes with their slender waists wrapped in yards of costly fabric. Day in and day out they tended to their low, black lacquered tables facing a flowerless garden of stone. It was dominated by smooth pebbles and two big, cone-shaped rocks which embodied tranquillity in the midst of a city.

The Chinese were represented as an endlessly marching army of starving children who took care of old parents. And there were young, brave people who challenged a brutal system with songs, speeches and bare hands on a square so large it could easily hold several villages, still the symbol of Chinese wealth. In the background was a wall so huge it could be seen from space. In their palaces stood tall, fragile vases encompassing thousands of years of art and tears.

Each immigrant had carried his own world of glory and terror, of love and fear within his worn body, mistreated by inadequate food during a long, dangerous sea voyage. Not everyone who left the old country got to the new world. Some had been buried at sea, the biggest grave of all.

Long before the Statue was built there had been the fate of African-American families. At first, loyalty to their white owners was beaten onto their backs. Then they were punished for the sake of duty and responsibility—the two prerequisites for leadership. Whose leadership? From the day he was born, the black man was made to feel a slave. Only his immense instinct for life enabled him to survive his lot.

It was not just his body that was shackled. Horses too have been deprived of their freedom. But only the most intelligent among these long-maned creatures have faint recollections of a flaming sky and no harness.

It was the black man's soul that was trampled upon and his mind was covered with a grimy hood that suffocated him. Every day he lived in fear his child and wife might be taken from him, sold to a stranger who drove away with them, not ever to be seen again. Not allowed to learn to read, he reverted to the ancient oral tradition, memorizing songs and prayers from generation to generation.

Doing so, he discovered music. He produced sounds never heard before, either in the old nor in the new world. He knew sad and wild tunes, sounds bursting from a heart so fierce and forlorn they could only be brought forth with swaying feet and clapping hands. He played with closed eyes and his fingers and wrists held instruments as tenderly as an infant. His body became his voice. While he sang and played his shackles fell off. He was free like the bird above his head. It was his only freedom.

The boy's mother preferred the Statue of Liberty to the elaborately painted saints who lived shyly under luxurious chandeliers in the numerous, stately churches of New York. Her son would be a fully grown man before he understood why she clung so fiercely to her Statue.

Inside the Statue it was a long climb upward. Sometimes the young woman got so tired and nauseated she could not help feeling it would be much easier to let herself simply slither down the many steps she had come up. Everything would be solved at once. All she had to do was to push the door with the red exit sign above it.

There were so many steps and each platform seemed to be just another landing that led on further. She got out of breath and could feel her heart beat as the years wore on and the end of the staircase was still not in sight. Several times she lost track of how far she had climbed. Each new set of stairs looked exactly the same and there were no windows as she had encountered them in the towers of European castles and churches. Without windows she was unable to measure her progress by looking outside. If her legs had not hurt and her breath not gotten shorter, she would not have believed she had gained any height at all. It seemed more as if she were going around in circles. How else could she have gotten so wobbly? Sometimes she thought, what if I reach the top and it will be blown away within moments of my arrival? Then she wept from sheer exhaustion.

Choking from tears and lack of air, she held on to the railing otherwise she would have fallen. She avoided looking down. She only had done so once. For a moment she had been unable to pull her head back up again. So quickly had it bent forward and become so heavy, it pulled her neck and torso over the railing. She almost lost her balance and tumbled into the void. It was as if she were being pushed by something stronger than her.

Looking down, she saw her body falling and becoming smaller and smaller until it disappeared into the abyss. Before she heard the deadly impact, she came to. Her stomach was retching. She screamed, then started to sob helplessly.

At other times it seemed to her she was not climbing upwards but down instead. Then she became frightened and was unable to inhale. She stood still, closed her eyes and imagined the glittering lights of Manhattan outside at the Statue's feet until she could breathe again. It took minutes before the spinning of her head with its maddening black and white movements that ceaselessly intertwined in sickening coils, discontinued. She knew she was aging quickly. It seemed to her that her youth had passed while she had momentarily blinked an eye. And she remembered the poet's voice,

"A woman's beauty is like a white
Frail bird, like a white sea-bird . . .
A sudden storm, and it was thrown
Between dark furrows upon the ploughed land . . ."

There were terrible moments during the young woman's life in New York, like those when her gaze was unable to get past the exit sign. At night when she could not sleep, it stood out in big red letters and lured her with a mocking smile that revealed pointed teeth.

There were good moments too like those when, almost

within reach of the exit sign, she also saw a pair of eyes. Their color was hard to tell. They were partly blue, partly gray, with a touch of hazel swimming in their midst as if a golden beaker had once been thrown into a bitter sea. The eyes belonged to her son as he had lain in swaddling clothes on his Armenian grandparent's soft bed in Ethiopia. He was six months old and his head, too large at birth, still dominated over his small, faultlessly formed body.

The boy's parents had just come back from their belated honeymoon which had been spent partly at Massava, one of two Ethiopian Red Sea ports. Since the young woman had given birth to her son only two months after her wedding, there had been no time to travel until the child was a few months old.

Before their trip, the baby had been put in his grandparents' care and upon his mother's return, he was asleep. The instant she walked softly through the door of the dull, cluttered bedroom, her son woke up as if he sensed her presence. Upon recognizing her, he smiled. To the mother it was as if an unknown sun rose from deep, shadowy precipices. The moment her son's smile touched the mountain tops, they lit up as if struck by fire. She had never seen this sun before and its light forced unknown chambers open in her. She felt then as if she had suddenly grown a few inches, as if something inside her, her intestinal tracts, her lungs, her heart, she did not know what, had become wider and larger. The smile was as if a wall in a house had been broken down to reveal large, secret rooms of gracious proportions. As long as she lived, she suddenly remembered this one smile of her small son. She needed to cling to it. His smile counterbalanced the numerous guilt feelings she had toward her children, toward her failed marriage, her own, difficult childhood and toward life in general.

Her son's smile pointed the way to a different universe from hers. To her his world was a frightening one because of its unknowable quality. The stars her son's smile illuminated would not be hers. Their very form which in her eyes looked more like saucers than the familiar egg-shaped ones, reminded her of a table-top earth, the flat one that had preceded the planets of Copernicus, Galilei and Kepler. For her satellites and spaceships were something too foreign to be acceptable. She did not like the almost total absence of plants, animals and water of the new planetaries. She loved hair too well to see the beauty of bald women and men as they walked in space. But she liked the absence of gasoline propelled engines and what might have been a car on earth. She also had no objection to people moving swiftly on four or eight wheels, the skaters and rollerbladers. And she enjoyed to watch the children who were, as usual, flowing with more natural grace and ease than the adults.

On the whole she preferred life on the star she was born on. The imagination of the boy's mother did not project the future. It worked more like a mole burrowing through dozens of somber underground paths where the past was stored. To conjure up life on a satellite or other celestial bodies beyond earth did not interest her much. She did not like the idea that the moon had been stepped upon. She respected scientific endeavors but would have preferred if the moon had been circumnavigated like a sacred island during the exploration of space.

She chose to dream about Chenauceau and its gray sheep grazing in a thick evening mist near the river. After so many years, she still saw their slow movements among tall trees. In her mind she continued to see the harmonious gestures of seven gardeners who worked together while the light faded fast. Slowly, the silhouettes of the sheep dissolved into large shadows. Their disappearance had filled her with a wild sadness only one human being could calm.

Where on a satellite would she find the black swan she had suddenly encountered in a forgotten bend of the Neckar? The river had barely reached her knees as she slowly waded with a hitched skirt through the mud of the stagnant water before she spotted the regal bird. For a moment the young girl and feathered creature had stood still in the warm river and looked at each other. Then the swan curved his snakelike, graceful neck even more and started to glide across the glistening surface of the water, away from her.

Where in space would she stumble among the ruins of a castle at the banks of the Rhine? Or be able to go to a solid, round tower, where a baron once had locked up his daughter for life? Inside the tower a pale, fragile girl had sat in solitude year after year because she preferred a young lover

33

to her father. Her father did not approve of her love. For ten years the girl was a captive of her father's phallic possession. A paternal maleness had grown into madness. And this Danae was not visited by Zeus. Pitifully she died. The tower became her tombstone. It still stands next to the Rhine.

With all her strength the boy's mother clung to the earth. Her son would conquer stars but she would stay within the sea. On moonlit nights she would continue to emerge and sing at the shore, her lower half hidden among sand and glistening rocks.

Then during a humid summer night in New York the young woman discovered that to be a mother meant to acknowledge one more defeat in her life. As she tossed and turned in her bed with nerves still raw from undigested events that had occurred during the day at work, she realized that the ideal of motherhood had been reinforced too early in her life. Its colors were too flamboyant not to cause another smashing of a golden mirror when it was confronted with bleak reality.

When she was five years old and lived in a small town in Southern Germany, she had found an art book in her absent father's library. The book was forbidden to be touched because its expensive color reproductions were not meant to be held by a child's dirty hand. Nobody had ever told her about Raphael yet she was drawn often to his Madonnas and child. At quiet moments she went to the heavy book and ran her fingers, as if reading Braille, across the prints. Her fingertips rather than her eyes, seemed to absorb the various shapes and forms. She liked to touch the smooth, thick, silky pages of the book. Of course she did smear the pages and even tore one of them. When the damage was discovered years later, it caused a fatherly temper tantrum that terrified her. But while she remained undiscovered, Raphael made her sit for years in the midst of roses where she fondled a fat, naked baby in her lap.

This happened before she saw herself holding hands with a handsome youth. She was a mother long before she walked with a lover along the shores of the Neckar and among pink and white clouds. Barely touching the boy's fingers, she felt encased in an eternal presence that only lasted until the next morning. Quite in line with Mary's immaculate conception, she saw herself attached to a child before she worried about the role a man played in it.

These dreams contrasted greatly with her actual experience as a baby sitter. She did not care about real babies and toddlers. They were always such a nuisance! They broke her toys. They cried at the wrong moments and they were unable to communicate. Contrary to the infants of the Madonnas who sat so daintily on long, silk skirts, real babies were so heavy one could hardly hold them on one's knees. If they fell, their screams caused their mothers to come running, mothers who then always asked questions she could not answer. And babies constantly misbehaved. In the midst of the nicest thoughts, they suddenly started to smell in a most obnoxious way. If one was not careful, some of their content flowed into one's hands. She soon learned to avoid babies altogether. It was a hundred times more pleasant to slip unseen into her father's room and chat with Raphael.

III

a mani libere
(unbound hands)

A divorcée in her early thirties and working in
Manhattan but living across the Hudson river in New Jersey,
the young woman considered wedlock once more. When she
failed in her attempt to get married again, she withdrew into
her shell with such anger in her heart that for months the
world swirled in purple and black around her. Almost every
sentence spoken to her during the day contained a word that
was innocent in itself, but when she brought it in context
with her rejected lover, she felt it was flung at her with
hostility. The very air seemed to contain tiny bits of flesh as
if by withdrawing too quickly behind closed doors, parts of
her skin had been caught between sharp edges and cut her to
the bone. The scent of blood drew sharks and other predatory
fish close to her house. After a while she became afraid to
leave for work in the morning.

Before her lover's departure there had been a horrible
last scene during which she had shut him out of her home.

More a cottage than a house, it had two modest bedrooms
and was built on a hilly acre of land that was good for sleigh
rides and her son's first attempts at skiing. Closed in by
shrubbery, it sat prettily across from a golf-course bordered
by tall, old trees, full of birds and squirrels. After each storm
broken branches and big chunks of brown bark lay on the
grass below them. The young woman taught her children
early to collect the dead wood and carry it behind the house

where a small forest was part of a neighbor's property. Later the old branches would be used to build a bonfire. At least that was always on everybody's mind. Several yards beyond the wide, unprotected terrace in front of the cottage where the heavy summer rains created a huge puddle the children loved to splash in, was a busy road. Hard to cut lawns were interrupted by a horseshoe shaped, gravel drive-way. Grass and trees created a safe distance from the cars that rushed to and from, usually above the speed limit.

It was early evening but already dark. The woman's lover, stronger and bigger than she, was in no mood to leave. She had barely been able to coax him through the front door when he tried to break in again. His violent and prolonged attempts to force the back door open and his struggle to climb in through windows of the one-story cottage frightened not only her, but also terrorized her children. With her five-year-old daughter holding on to her and crying loudly, the woman screamed into the phone for the police. Her slightly older son clung to her skirt. His face was distorted by fear and his eyes were becoming enlarged like those of a cat in the dark.

Horrified by the kicks the woman's infuriated lover administered to the wooden kitchen door, mother and children ran from room to room to make sure all windows were closed. For what seemed like hours, they waited and feared the police would get to the house too late.

When the man she had considered marrying managed to put his hands inside the green screen of her bedroom window and tried to pull himself through it, the woman slammed the wooden frame as hard as she could on his fingers. He howled with pain and rage, then swore at the woman in the most obscene and threatening language imaginable. She felt as if a pot full of scalding water had been thrown into her face. With hate and apprehension she watched him holding his hand as he hobbled away from the small house. Half hidden by tall trees the cottage sat in the dark and seemed to absorb part of the drama displayed in its interior.

Shortly after the woman had hurt the man's fingers, she heard his footsteps again. As he started to rattle at another window, she listened fearfully. Where, for God's sake, is the police, she thought again. When she finally saw the police car pull up the driveway, her heart stopped fluttering like a frightened bird. She knew they were out of immediate danger. For the first time she was able to lift up her whimpering daughter and cradle her in her arms. The small boy put both of his arms around his mother's waist and hid his face in her clothes. All three of them were crying.

The two young police officers with their broad rimmed hats stood calmly in front of the kitchen stove. Carefully, even gently, they began to question the woman and her lover, who by now had been escorted back into the house. In spite of the officers' consideration, the young woman felt one wave of shame after another running across her. While her children hung onto her hips wailing, she was burned again and again as if someone continued to pour boiling water over her head. Each question stung her more. She tried to be outwardly as coherent as possible, but she knew her words made little sense. She was painfully aware of her disarrayed hair and clothes. The woman's lover was at first oblivious to what she experienced as a public exposure. But when he saw her red face and became aware of her humiliation, he began to enjoy her distress. Revenge was on his mind. Far from experiencing guilt or shame he continued to disregard blatantly the waiting officers. As slowly as possible, he collected his personal belongings. How friendly these American police men are, the young woman thought who had experienced much less patient guardians of the law in Europe and Africa. As a child in Germany, she had learned to fear all uniforms.

The woman's lover moved as if he had been intoxicated and continued to hurdle in a subdued voice insults and accusations at her. Several times she looked beseechingly at the officers, but either they did not hear him or pretended not to notice anything. For them the scene that hurt her so deeply was a routine call. The domestic quarrel they witnessed was in their eyes, used to more weighty crimes, nothing serious. For the woman it was as if she had been caught in a nightmare. Try as she might she could not wake up.

Walking aimlessly back and forth between kitchen and living room, temporarily shaking off her children like a she-wolf who has to get ready for yet another fight, she noticed her lover's voice had suddenly started to drawl. His words became barely audible to her. It was as if the speed of a record player had been reduced so the sounds started to be stretched as if pulled by a rubber band. His sadistic words that a moment ago had bitten the woman now, in their distortion, had a funny edge to it that made her smile.

Then she noticed that the dark-blue uniforms of the officers were changing into a grayish-pink hue. Worse yet, their fresh faces had become twice as large and their heads resembled two full moons suspended side by side, benevolently shining upon their surroundings.

Strangest of all, she realized the tears on her small daughter's face, which she had wiped off several times now seemed to glow with such brilliance that she tried to collect them in her hand as if they had been pearls. Yet before she could touch them they rolled away from her and disappeared.

Shortly afterward the woman heard a voice murmur softly, then break into a singsong. The unintelligible sounds which escaped from her lips seemed partly to be torn prayers, partly forgotten parts of a lullaby. For a while she was unaware that it was her own voice that sang and whispered broken-heartedly.

Later the woman found herself sitting on the floor in a corner, holding both her children close to her. They had finally stopped crying and were falling asleep. The small house was calm. A low hanging tree branch brushed faintly against the squatty roof. The woman's lover had left.

Their quarrel had started quite harmlessly. It was a Friday night and the children, the woman and the man were sitting on the couch in the little, square living room, watching television. Her son was on her right, her lover on her left. For quite a while he had held the woman's daughter, who was his favorite, on his lap.

It was just before the children's bed time. Everyone was tired at the end of a hard week. Most of the evening her son, a healthy child, had been weeping as if he were coming down with a cold. In a quarrelsome voice and with little moans the child had complained while she fed and bathed him. It had not helped calm down an atmosphere ready to burst with tired nerves that seemed to be strung on almost visible wires throughout the cottage.

Too tired to control the situation fully, the woman had watched the man, who was considerably older than she and not used to children, grow more and more irritable. She dreaded him losing his temper. He was of Italian descent and his rages were violent, filled with foul invectives, hurled at her like fistfuls of feces. Until the woman met him, she had not known what gutter language was. In the beginning of their fights when he threw four letter words at her, she felt as if he had smeared her face with excrement. It made her stomach heave. Sometimes late at night when the young woman was exhausted, her angry tears mixed with vomit.

The young woman knew she was too tired to handle one of the man's rages tonight. Her daughter already tried to help and please whenever possible. She attempted to outrun everyone on her swift legs, still short but already shaped exquisitely. The little girl was keenly aware of the tension building up between the two adults who towered above her. Small as she was she attempted to alleviate the atmosphere in her own sweet way. How lucky I am to have her, the young woman thought as she kept her son's whimpers as unobtrusive as possible. I have good children, she reflected again, trying hard not to let exhaustion get the upper hand.

Finally they had settled down next to each other on the sofa. The woman's son had snuggled up to her. With burning cheeks, getting sleepy, he looked at the screen. Wanting to rock her son who suddenly looked so small to her, she refrained from it. She did not want to further arouse the Italian's jealousy. He had little objection when she hugged her dark-eyed daughter, but had tried several times to get between her and her son when she held him close. The young woman felt her son, only a year and a half older than his sister, needed her affection as much as his pretty sibling.

But the Italian did not agree. In his presence the young woman was only allowed to measure out her love, by the spoonful, to her son. Their different views on child-raising had caused most of their fights among them, some of which had become terrible and ugly.

Later the young woman could not recall how the battle had started. Perhaps her son had said one more wrong word at the wrong moment or said it in a particularly obnoxious voice. But at one point before she could prevent it, the

Italian unexpectedly reached across her waist and gave her son a fierce push. Taken by surprise the little boy toppled over and fell on the floor where, at first speechless, he started to scream. He was not hurt, but his mother, without thinking lurched herself against the Italian. Blindly, she put both hands around his throat and started to strangle him with all her strength, digging her long nails into his flesh. With a catlike movement the women's small daughter had slid out of the Italian's arms. Horror stricken she watched from a distance the foul struggle of the two adults. Neither child had ever witnessed a physical assault by their mother before. She simply did not do such things. Her German upbringing had not condoned bodily violence. It was considered vulgar and low class and most of all perhaps it evoked the ghosts of a recent, brutal past.

Even though the Italian had begun to cough and gasp for air, it was not long before he had sprung to his feet, thrown the woman against the wall and attempted to pin her arms behind her back. The moment his neck was out of her reach, she had tried to scratch and kick him. Alternatively, she shrieked for help and accused the Italian of trying to kill her son. "I hate you, I hate you, you butcher," she shouted again and again.

The man, who saw the woman had lost her senses, did not like the murderous glint in her eyes. He hated her tongue when it became a knife that stabbed him without compunction. Her mouth suddenly seemed to be able to roll words into sharp stones and fling them at him.

But it was her howling that frightened him the most. His own violence was subdued by this fear he was not able to overcome. Regaining his reason, he tried to calm her down. He knew the woman's cries would sooner or later bring people onto the scene. He disliked this idea intensely. He thought it wiser to obey the woman's persistent demands to leave her premises and reluctantly went outside the house. As soon as she saw him leave, she quickly locked front and back doors after him, telling her children to close all windows. Then, while the Italian begged to be let back into the house, she called the police.

During the rest of the night the young woman hardly slept. With ears strained to the utmost, she dreaded the returning footsteps of the Italian.

He never came back. Not as a lover. When he did return, he tried over many years to become a friend. He almost succeeded, since the woman was nearly alone in a new continent. He surrounded her with limitless patience and persistence. He then reminded her of uninhabited steppes where she ran across dry, stony ground, losing her breath and temper. Yet in spite of a considerable amount of education, his mind was too set in narrow moral conceptions. They had little to do with the young woman's. And not having raised children of his own, he never learned to cope with their needs.

What disturbed her perhaps the most was his prejudice when it came to people whose skin was a shade darker than his own. Suffering from xenophobia, he was also jealous. One of his favorite insults was to call his mistress a nigger lover.

"Why don't you marry one of them if you like them so much," he said, quickly attacking her on a personal level when she tried to defend an African American she had met at work or in one of her college classes. His eyes looked at her as if they had been replaced with two burning coals, their blackness surrounded by loud streaks of red. They separated menacingly from the white of his face. "You are just plain stupid," he said.

Jews did not fare much better than African Americans. With a sharp tongue he painted one ugly picture after another and forced her to look at it.

"I want to educate you," he claimed with religious conviction. She saw him standing on a soap box in London's Hyde Park where he drew a curious crowd ready to mock him. She too wanted to make fun of him but did not dare. She only exploded after he had verbally abused her to a point where she felt pushed into a tight, airless corner. During those horrible moments it was as if a heavy, red curtain suddenly descended in front of her eyes, trapping her so she could no longer breathe. Then she blindly lashed out, possessing a strength that rose from crevices within her she did not know existed. She was no longer in control of things. Her arms and legs flailed out as if obeying a command outside her body. Her tongue too found unfamiliar words. Something indigestible and poisonous like moth balls formed between her teeth and tongue. If she did not want to choke, she had to spit them out. "How can anybody be so narrow-minded and dumb," she screamed. "It is you who is an idiot not I," she repeated herself angrily.

During the days she remained calm, he lectured her in no uncertain terms:

"You are a Pollyanna and too naive to see beyond your nose." Then he spoon-fed her:

"I want to make you worldly! Don't you see? I am a teacher." When he understood his patronizing efforts were useless, he got angry and started to swear. The sallow color of his face turned a bluish-red and he lowered his head, becoming a bull ready to attack his tormentor. As she, at the last second, turned her hips, he crashed past her, missing her by an inch. From the momentum of his onslaught he fell over his own legs. But before she knew it, he had turned around. He reappeared out of the dusty distance that had swallowed him. Under her anxious eyes he became even more furious from an ever increasing rage now mixed with humiliation. "You bitch! I am going to teach you yet," he yelled, now with a white face.

It never occurred to him he might be wrong. He only saw her as a stubborn, arrogant German. In his eyes the young woman was someone incapable of making it in the world. Not for lack of intelligence, for even he recognized, usually in front of a few common friends, she had a good mind.

Yet a day did not pass without him accusing her that she closed her eyes to reality. His allegations had a strange effect on her. When he called her names, as he did even in front of the children, increasing her agony, she did close her eyes and try to see herself as a water lily whose long, snake-like stem wound itself protectively around her son and daughter. Yet the same stalk attempted to strangle the Italian. "One day I am going to kill you," she thought with a strange calmness.

His point of view, based on newspaper reports, talks with his colleagues at school, and television was the right one. His inamorata's opinion was not. When she did not agree with him, she caused him real anguish.

"I take pity on you. I am a teacher," he argued and believed it himself. "No one else wants you. If it were not

43

for me, you would have nobody to look after you and your kids," he hurdled many times at her head. In spite of his crude words that cut her, he saw himself as a knight rescuing his damsel.

In the young woman's eyes, he made her look like a blind beggar sitting in front of a medieval church door, barely covered in rags. Seeing herself like that she ground her teeth and was unable to swallow the moth balls in her mouth.

The Italian was a man with a heart but without tact. He constantly confused honesty with rudeness. He took pride in his bluntness. Carelessly, he made his abrasive comments even after one summer when New York high school teachers went on strike for three months and they lived on the young woman's small salary during that time.

Every night when she came home from work, he sat in the kitchen and waited for her. Dinner was ready but the children were not allowed to eat until she was home. If she missed her bus, the evening ended in utter misery.

Similar to her husband, the Italian understood love only in terms of possession and even though he taught math and history to young teenagers, he had no insights into a child's psyche. He would have made an inadequate father. Also, the woman could neither forget where he came from, nor that debasing night when she threw him out of her house. Images of this evening lingered with her. They seemed to have penetrated her skin and festered among nerves and tendons like worms.

Whenever the young woman reflected upon her and her lover's fate she saw that the roots of the dark-haired Italian were embedded in the pre-Christian era when Caligula and Claudius intermingled and when lives hung on the fingertips of Messalina. It was the time when the old Seneca, Nero's tutor, was forced by his former pupil to commit suicide because the mad Emperor had grown jealous of his influence. Sadly, she realized that once more she had chosen a man whose background and upbringing were totally different from her own. "He resembles a great deal your Armenian husband, except that he is older," her sister told the young woman one day.

The Italian's emotions had run unchecked during the many years he had spent as a bachelor. Part of that time had

44

been used to turn himself into a recluse in the best of Stoic examples. At one point he had for weeks on end not left his room. His food was brought to him by a dedicated girlfriend so he could finish his master thesis. He had felt it necessary to impose this austerity upon himself without which he would not have been able to reach his goal: to teach history and mathematics at a high school in Harlem.

The young woman's lover was the son of an immigrant from southern Italy who owned a bakery in Brooklyn. As a child he had worked in his father's shop. At eighteen he joined the Army. At the end of World War Two, he was employed as a car insurance investigator. He earned his two college degrees at night. It took him ten years. During that time he turned himself into a member of the respected middle class, the backbone of America.

In his moments of glory the Italian felt like Napoleon when he took the massive golden crown out of the pope's hand and placed it on his own head. Yet beneath his self-made vision, he could not forget his humble origin and remained insecure. Not until he was an old man did he forgive his father. Most of his life he had hated him because his father had forced him to help him at his store every day after school, depriving him of friends and play. His harsh childhood smoldered within him. He was envious of every small boy who was allowed to play baseball and participate in other sports. There were many reasons why he was jealous of the young woman's son.

At the end of a day, the end of his energy, and with the help of wine or whiskey, flames among the ashes often quickly leaped up in a last destructive dance. Alcohol did not agree with him. He became nasty when he was intoxicated.

It took several months after the young woman and her lover had broken up before she regained her fragile stability. It would most properly have taken considerably longer had she not accidentally met someone else.

* * *

Around 10:00 a.m. every morning a coffee wagon was pushed down most of the long, narrow marble floors of the forty story high office building she worked in. It was one of those elaborate edifices Manhattan is famous for. A block long entrance hall with a forty foot ceiling was furnished with a row of splendid chandeliers. Carpeted elevators led to various floors. At first a little intimidated by an army of guards wearing much gold braid, the young woman quickly got used to them and occasionally enjoyed exchanging a few words with them. Guards and coffee wagon soon became part of her environment. She always noticed a new face emerging from an unknown office. She was on amicable terms with everyone who stood in line waiting for coffee. When she observed a stranger, she was often the first one to offer a greeting. It was easier with women but some men were approachable without their mistaking her friendliness for something else. One morning she discerned a new face. It was attached to the tall, handsome figure of a man she found instantly attractive.

The stranger was tailored in the best of the New England tradition. And, as she soon discovered, he had two solid generations of Princeton behind him. It was not long either before she found out with the help of Armanda, his secretary, that he owned a plant in Terryville where he manufactured office furniture. One day Armanda also mentioned casually that he and his wife owned a three-story Tudor style house in Armonk, Westchester. Then the young woman learned that his exquisitely furnished home was surrounded by several, carefully tended acres of land including a wooden cottage in the midst of a small forest that grew wildly. On the property was a corral for horses where his teenage daughter kept a brown pony. "His marriage is on the rocks and his wife is an alcoholic," Armanda announced three weeks later when the two women ran into each other in the ladies room.

Physically too the stranger who had by now totally captivated the young woman's mind, was the embodiment of a *Wasp* dream. Slim, blue-eyed and light-haired with a matching beard she only knew in the form of stubbles, he had the long legs of a runner rather than those of a football player. His was a rosy skin stretching tightly over symmetrical features with a strong chin that promised to keep its impeccable line even in old age.

But next to his irresistible assets sweeping her off the

road like the torrential rains in East Africa that were capable of setting heavily loaded trucks afloat, ran a rivulet. It was narrow, yet deep, like the fact that he was barely separated from his wealthy wife and two children whom the young woman never met. She did get to know the many rooms of his house though and her children rode occasionally the young, docile horse waiting in the stable.

The Princeton man had just left home and was living at his aunt's New York apartment on Park Avenue. The elderly aunt took a liking to the young woman and accepted her children. She was fond of her nephew and wanted him to be happy. If happiness meant an affair with a German rather than trying to rescue a marriage that had become a raft caught in a hazardous, reef-rich undertow, this elderly, sophisticated New Yorker would not stand in her nephew's way.

The aunt's taste in clothes was impeccable. Her dresses were like stems of a flower crowned by golden petals. Blond-haired with an almost wrinkle-free face at age seventy, she moved her thin body with the grace of a dancer among the dark antique furniture with which her apartment was inundated.

At the right occasion the aunt, in the best tradition of a good fairy, provided the young woman with a sumptuous dress and matching pearls. A long, black gown demanded a white, short necklace.

The aunt's only objection to the young woman was a few extra pounds visible in the wrong places. Standing in the middle of her elaborate, cluttered living room, her eyes were brimming with criticism as they ran over the woman's figure whom she had asked to be presented to her in a tight, elegant dress. She stated her displeasure with raised eyebrows and a hardly audible sentence. But she made it as plain as if she had applied a cane to the glowing flesh in front of her that she regarded women who were unable to control their weight an inferior breed. No matter what age or upbringing.

The aunt's criticism, undoubtedly well meant, had disastrous results. The young woman was already overwhelmed by the aunt's unexpected generosity and the unaccustomed refinements of New York whose brilliance and superficiality had charmed her. Miserable, she was only able to see herself as the distorted reflection in the eyes of the aunt.

The young woman's anticipation of an unavoidable dinner dance at a Westchester country club turned into a grotesque image in which she saw herself stumbling upon the seam of her long, rustling garment and toppling headlong on a slippery floor. Her fall reverberated across the surface of the large room and caused ripples of laughter among the other guests. Most of them sat daintily at the edge of the highly polished dance floor. The women's costly robes trailed on the ground and made it difficult for the waiters not to step on them. On every table stood tall champagne glasses next to a vase with yellow roses. And there were thin china plates of all sizes and pastel colors.

Her beau would, of course, be infinitely embarrassed by her unheard of clumsiness and for the rest of the night drown his sorrow in whiskey.

When they did arrive at the dance, her escort looked splendid in a tuxedo and a dazzling smile. But the young woman escaped into the ladies room where she stayed for a considerable time. Without getting tired, she rearranged her hair and make-up that had been put on with professional skill. She saw herself sitting at the hairdresser's again where she had procrastinated her stay and listened with a sick stomach to the compliments of the coiffeur because she did not want to go home and get dressed for the party. She rather risked her Princeton man getting impatient with her for the first time. "What kept you? We have a long ride," he said before they rushed off in the car. For a moment she thought she smelled a faint breath of whiskey coming from his mouth.

She looked lovely and far from being stupid, she was usually one of the visual points of any large social gathering. But it was obvious that she had little self-confidence. Even the most banal sentences made her feel uncomfortable. She had a talent to read into a simple remark negative connotations that did not exist. That night, only after a prolonged conversation with an elderly lady, who was delighted to have an impromptu, attentive listener at a dance, and after several rounds of turbulent moves with her Princeton man on the parquet floor, did the young woman start to enjoy herself a little. By that time it had become late. Most guests were in an advanced state of happiness caused by music, laughter and wine. The latter made her feel left out again since she hardly drank.

Her shyness was bound to her most immediate environment. While still married, she had attended and given parties in East Africa next to which the dinner dance at the Westchester club looked no longer imposing. But those affairs had been arranged with the help and sometimes supervision of her husband. They included some of his family members whose eyes and arms gave her the support she thought she did not need.

Where in East Africa and during her marriage she was assisted in too solicitous a manner, in New York she encountered the reverse. Even though it was not true, she felt she had to take every step on her own.

* * *

At first when she arrived in the United States, the young woman had hated Manhattan. It took her two years to get used to the manners, or rather the lack of it, of most New Yorkers. Nobody said "please" or "thank you." Phone operators got instantly insolent when she asked them to repeat a number or spell a name. Used to the *King's English* she had been taught at the German gymnasium and while she lived in England, she often had difficulties understanding people from Brooklyn. When someone told her that her children spoke English well and had acquired a New Jersey accent, she broke into tears. She wanted them to speak like her even though she was highly self-conscious of her German and British inflection. At work she was often on the telephone and invisible strangers frequently asked her to repeat a name or an address she needed. She knew some employees of the various companies she dealt with did this just so that she would keep talking. It made her angry but she did not dare to show her frustration. She was icily polite and New Yorkers kept pushing her to repeat herself. It was a game she eventually learned to play. When she discovered that the brusqueness of New Yorkers was just skin deep and underneath they were people like all others, she snapped back at them. That won her respect. But she never got used to abrupt behavior.

In the evening, whenever the young woman had enough energy left and picked-up sufficient courage to get herself out of the cottage in New Jersey she and her children rented for several years, she went alone. This was not easy after a long day at work, taking care of her children, the house and attending college classes a night. The young woman could only bring herself to go to an event in which her children were involved. It was usually within the circle of a small suburban church or some type of sporting event in which her son or her daughter participated.

Even to do this, she had to use a strong image projecting what the evening might be like. This reflection was like a balloon she released outside her kitchen door. While she watched the gas-filled body slowly rise toward the delicate sickle of a newly born moon, she ran down her front steps, started the engine of her old car and with her eyes following the now almost invisible balloon, she went into the night.

Even accompanied by a friend who gave her emotional support, or escorted on the gallant arm of a paramour, it was not the same as it had been with her husband in Ethiopia. She had always looked down upon convention. She saw herself as a free spirit somehow floating above it. Now she paid the penalty of having done so. Without noticing it, she had become a creature of habit and rules. She woke up one morning and discovered she was no longer interested in fighting the fashion of the day. If a husband was socially more acceptable within her most immediate circle than a lover, she was no longer interested in opposing this requirement.

This was a sad conclusion though she realized it only through a dark glass wall at the time. She had become a gray mare who pulled without protest the opinions and moral convictions of her environment. The halter and bridle had broken her down. With docility she accepted the oppressiveness and rigidity of institutions with which she had little in common.

With time her temper tantrums, a dark paternal gift, got more violent than ever. One morning after a long bus ride into New York and during her quick walk to work, she suddenly became aware she had started to pay more attention to crazy people, visible in the corners of skyscrapers, next to their sumptuous entrances. She felt that like them she was being swept along Manhattan's swift current as if she too had been one of the dead pigeons she saw thrown to the side. Her eyes were mostly cast down and heeded nothing but scurrying feet. But she saw that by instinct everyone tried not to step on the dead bird or one of its gray wings.

The mad people were easy to spot since they announced their whereabouts with wild shrieks that were sometimes accompanied by an impaired gait and gesticulating arms. One of the demented figures was a woman with an attractive figure who moved with the silence of a cat. She wore a mask of the most violent colors. Her eyelids and white cheekbones were dabbed with huge blotches of black and blue. And her mouth was a purple gap blinking with a set of sharp teeth. Her face had become a silent scream. In it, two eyes flitted back and forth in restless horror. This woman, still young and far better dressed than the other deranged human beings, frightened her the most. It was one of the distorted mirror images New York threw out to her in such abundance. It forced her to take a close look at herself.

In order to offset her fear, she quickly visualized a small, golden mirror held by a Cupid. Reflected in it was one of Velazquez' most charming faces supported by a long neck and the perfectly drawn line of a woman's back. Languidly the nude lay on a couch. The dazzling white of the woman's skin that contrasted with such elegance against a black velvet cloth, consoled her for a short while.

Whereas before the young woman had hurried past New York's concrete forms of insanity averting her eyes, she now, as if pulled by an invisible string, deliberately slowed down her steps while following one of the unfortunate creatures. This enabled her to take in their movements before they became aware of her watching them. The moment she passed one of them, she slowly turned around in order to get a full view of their faces. If the features showed uncountable wrinkles, matched by gray or white hair that fell in greasy strings on hunched-over shoulders, she was less shocked, as if old age and psychotic behavior went hand in hand. But if a deranged face, especially a female one, was young, she felt

51

someone had viciously boxed her ear and she became momentarily stunned from pain and humiliation. Swaying left and right, as if she were intoxicated and not sure if she were going to fall, she hurried on until she got out of breath.

Sometimes rather than being terrified, she was aware of some sort of envy for these unhappy beings. In her confused state of mind, she thought their suffering gave them privileges denied to sane people. She then was drawn toward the crazy men and women she encountered on the street. Eagerly she wanted to enter their magic garden of beasts which allowed them to escape from the obligations and daily chores with which her own life was so heavily burdened. In her trance-like state, she imagined times and countries where the insane were not abused but treated gently as if they had been saints.

Another social obstacle was the young woman's innate shyness she was not able to overcome. Still lithe in her mid-thirties, if not more so than at twenty, she no longer craved the limelight and brilliant colors she had courted during her adolescence in Germany when she had wanted an audience. Like most adolescents she had challenged her elders. Only slowly over many years and with outside help did she learn to use subtle colors. As she discovered, they underlined her own person rather than the latest style in clothes and maquillage she used to advertise. Insecure yet vain, the woman had always felt the need to be distinguished from others.

* * *

As a young girl in Europe, she had sometimes accomplished a certain amount of detachment by surrounding herself with mirrors and candles that showed her center stage. Every now and then she wore a bright red dress whose low cut decolleté offered herself as if she had been one of the apples and roses lovers like to gather. Beyond the limelights of the stage, the onlookers were not recognizable as individuals but only as the dark surface of a pond at night. Rarely did a familiar face appear at different spots like a forgotten water lily. The lights blinded her. If her friends did not call her name, she did not know they were among the crowd.

When the young girl was in a more playful rather than a foolish, heroic mood, and still craved attention with the clumsy voluptuousness of a twenty-year-old, she thought of another trick, like putting a tamed white mouse with a pink tail on her shoulder. Sometimes she did this while dancing closely entwined with a tall, well-proportioned youth. Once she was accompanied to an elegant German nightclub whose small dance floor was surrounded by hardly any lights at all. Thick carpets spread everywhere except under ones dancing feet. The music was muted and permitted the dancers to sway sensuously back and forth. The rhythmic movement induced a dreamlike state. Everybody, young and old, wore a beatific expression and seemed to spin in their own worlds of evanescent dreams. The men and women resembled empty seashells cast upon the shore. The blissful state lasted until someone saw the mouse.

The mouse, happy to be freed from a tiny evening handbag or a deep trouser pocket, started to scurry back and forth. It frantically tried to submerge from shoulders into lower regions. Its appearance never failed to produce hushed shrieks from the carefully painted mouths of women and rather loudly voiced protests from men. Sounds of frustration and anger and the shuffling of feet hurrying to safety came particularly from those closest to herself and her partner. The revelers thought they were hallucinating on account of the alcohol they had consumed. The stares the young girl received were far from being admiring, but she had accomplished what she came for: She had been noticed. Little did she know then that only a few years later she would crave invisibility.

* * *

Head of her small household at thirty-five, the young woman had mastered the elementary rules for survival in the United States. It was the third continent she had made her home. Though born and raised in Germany, she had experienced prolonged stays in England, France and Italy. At the age of twenty-two, she had moved to East Africa, married and quickly given birth to two children. The woman and her family lived for seven years in Ethiopia.

Now having finally come close to maturity, she shrank more and more away from people. She loved mankind as an abstract entity, as something she conversed with on a large level. When it came to a strange individual, she felt ill at ease. At the end of a day, she sought solace in the silky fur of her cat. As the years fled in front of her like leaves blown by a playful autumn wind, she searched more and more for the voices of her daughter and son rather than the sounds of a lover or potential marriage candidate.

Growing older she wanted total effacement, total absorption in her environment. She imagined what it would be like if her comings and goings were only noticed like the odor of a flower or fruit. She would have liked to have turned into a sort of walking plant in bloom but transparent, so people only became aware of her after she had passed them and they had inhaled her scent.

Her longing for affection was constant but she did not want to be touched or even spoken to directly. She respected the fishbowls in which she saw the heads of New Yorkers encased while they walked in the pungent sunlight falling off the cliffs of Fifth Avenue. But she could not understand why strangers wanted to hold her, to squeeze her between their hands as if her flesh were eatable. To her, it was quite enough to run one's fingers lightly over the skin as if reading braille.

For her to touch was not just a pleasure for its own sake, but a means by which one was able to read entire pages of people whose meaning had been for a long time almost inaccessible. Fingertips were supposed to lead into the blind chambers of the heart. Imperceptibly, they were meant to explore those places where the winds of bitterness had blown a thousand years and where the different shapes of fear moved silently like animals stalking their prey.

To her the human heart was raw and messy. It was a wound barely healed. Its edges were coagulated with blood, debris and dirt and only faintly, like an early morning light, had music touched upon it. She wanted to see, not to be seen. Yet she needed recognition and affection.

She was afraid of love. She knew what its pain felt like. For sex she cared little, unless her emotions were involved. It was not that the magnificent male body did not excite her.

On the contrary! She got carried away by a noble head and well-shaped limbs. There was hardly a greater delight than to lightly touch strong, healthy muscles under a sun-tanned skin. Her eyes and mouth traveled with pleasure from north to south and east to west until she knew most of the body's anatomy. She inhaled with pleasure the various scents that belonged to different places and corners. And always self-conscious, she allowed her hands to follow her nose, walking up and down hills of biceps and sinews.

What thrilled her less was a high concentration on the sexual organs only. Hair was a type of protein she did not crave. She felt the garden surrounding a mansion should only be moved through slowly, not to be made an abode of its own. To appreciate the fleeting beauty of flowers, she did not need to claw the earth and assure herself of the size and color of its roots. Earth and hair in her mouth did not stimulate her. It prevented her from enjoying more delicate odors.

Once inside the manor, she gladly threw herself into its milk-colored pool and delighted in the vigorous strokes that rocked her back and forth. Slowly, and in a rather precise manner as if playing Telemann, she moved from one end of the pool to the next. Since she considered herself a long distance swimmer, she cared little for speed. Swimming back and forth endless numbers of times restored her strength. It put her into a hypnotic state of mind that superseded rational thoughts. The exercise brought color to her pale cheeks and forced her to breathe thoroughly, the way one was meant to inhale.

Yet in the end, lovemaking was restricted by the monotony of the same moves. If executed with the rhythm of the sea, and if capable of adjusting one's own rhythm to the same heartbeat as one's partner so one could attempt, while still in the water, to perform a *pas de deux*, it was, so she was told by experts, one of the most enjoyable exercises man could know. Of course, she would have to overcome the flatness of loveplay, the ceaseless rocking back and forth like surf on sand. To her the moves of love were similar to those of work. It was like two of these huge, heavy-footed, patient horses pulling a wagon of hundreds of gallons of beer. They must pass along the same street many times before they are

55

able to remember each door, each window with its various potted flowers that nod in rhythm with their hooves.

She was also told lovemaking was an art. It took a little while to learn—about a thousand years, give or take. Yet any small progress is instantly rewarded and those who become skillful at it, vow there is no greater pleasure.

After many years and innumerable, embarrassing errors when making love, the woman discovered she did no longer lack skill but the right man. Where was Adam of whom—the Church insisted in spite of Darwin and other scientists—she had once been a part. Where was her missing half, the other smooth-skinned human back, Diotima had sung about so persistently?

IV

Erratum
(Mistake)

When the bachelor, as a middle-aged man, looked back upon his mother's third marital attempt, he, with the advantage of hind sight, could only then understand why it was not possible for his mother to marry again. He was sure it had less to do with the men she encountered than with her own state of mind. After her unhappy first attempt among the solitary mountains of Ethiopia, his mother was so afraid of the tight bonds of marriage that her choice fell without failure upon a man little suited to marry her.

She felt her marriage had reinforced her weakness and ugliness. Her strong sides were closed off as if the pen with which she signed her marriage license had been able to channel a river into an irrigation system. The water that before had run wildly with white crowns perched on every rock over which the river tumbled, was now divided into hundreds of pipes whose content helped to fertilize fields. Her courage, paired with an inexhaustible curiosity had led her to explore territories closed off to more timid minds. Then one day her river had been metamorphosed into water faucets a child could turn off or on with the slightest touch of its hand. The price for civilization had been too high.

Sometimes during a cold mountain night in Addis Ababa when the young woman could not sleep, she lay on her vast bed and listened. Soon she heard steady drops of water falling into her kitchen sink. After a short while the sound threatened to drive her insane because she imagined somewhere behind the faucet and inside thousands of feet of pipe, her river, the part of her she loved best, still roared. Now, unless she became a water rat, she could no longer swim in it. Cruelly she had been fastened to a bed, a room, a house, a husband and children. The young woman knew how Gulliver felt when he woke up one morning and could no longer move his head because his hair had been tied to the seashore with hundreds of strings.

The bachelor's father was a shrewd, hard-working businessman with a large office in the center of Addis Ababa. His head was swirling with figures from morning till night. And he handled with charisma customers speaking French, Italian, English, Amharic and Armenian. But even though he was bright and skilled in his trade, he could not comprehend the restlessness of his wife. In his abortive attempts to fathom her, he said again and again:

"I do not understand you! You have everything you need. A house, a car, domestic help, children and a husband! What more do you want?"

His wife never knew how to answer this question he started to ask more and more frequently. Without a word she looked at him, then shrugged her shoulders and walked away. She had been cast for marriage by a two-thousand-year-old tradition. She had also been encouraged by her parents to become independent, to work hard at her education, so she would be able to stand on her own feet if her marriage failed.

Her father, whose mind was large enough to not only encompass the present but also future events, was painfully aware that his daughter's generation was different from his own. There had been so many changes. He was conscious that after two world wars during which women from all corners of the earth were needed to take over men's jobs, they fought more successfully for their rights. They grew more ambitious. He was not sure if he could cope with that. Especially after 1945, when women became disturbed by being second class citizens, he grew more and more upset. He did not like it when slowly several women started to speak. And he detested Simone de Beauvoir when she evolved into the voice for thousands of women who rallied behind her. As they tried to storm the bastions of patriarchy, he felt threatened.

The woman's father took delight in his daughter's endurance during sportive events, such as strenuous ski excursions. And he enjoyed her company under an open sky. But at home where he constantly felt under stress, he became tyrannical.

It was her mother who was largely in control of events taking place under their roof. She was an accomplished hostess and dancer who noticed early on, her daughter's lack of those skills. At social events the mother became aware that the daughter did not move gracefully to music. The young girl had difficulties adjusting her own rhythm to those of her partners, especially the older ones. She wanted to lead rather than being led. She did not pace her steps with those of the young men with whom she danced. They were usually exciting to look at with their first fluffy mustaches shading their upper lips, but it was obvious she would have preferred if they had followed her rather than she them.

* * *

Now, a few years later after the mother of the bachelor had settled in Ethiopia and reflected on her husband's angry words, she knew she did not want more from her marriage. If anything, she wanted less when it came to her physical surroundings. What she desired was a dream she had cherished as an adolescent. True, it was a gigantic dream, an oversized shadow that scorned human dimensions. Yet stubbornly she clung to it. Not realizing for a long time there could be no escape from materialism and that her own body even more than her husband's pulled her cruelly to the ground, she had hoped marriage would let her walk hand in hand with the man she loved. Like Chagall's *Bride and Bridegroom* she had seen her beloved and herself float above red roof tops and beyond the mountains until they reached the sea and the invisible borderline that separates earth from sky.

In the afternoon, during the early days of her marriage, as she sat alone in her silent, darkened living room among the African mountains, she spun herself into a cocoon where she appeared with long, wind-blown hair still damp from the sea

59

whose gentle waves had carried her to the shore. The facial features of the male figure approaching her did not necessarily bear any resemblance with those of her husband. This did not matter since her phantasies were innocent like those of a child and did not go beyond walking at the shore, holding hands. Even after five years of marriage and two children she had not yet discovered the art of having an orgasm during intercourse. Nor did she know what masturbation was about. She had been taught that only men stimulated their genital organs manually. And even they risked, she was told, of becoming blind during the process. *Amour solitaire*, an American teaching French poetry at the Haile Selassie I University where her husband finally allowed her to attend, had called it. Her professor was the first person whom she had heard speaking objectively about this embarrassing mystery. And his eyesight was perfect.

To the young woman's husband whose mind had been engaged most of the day working out long, complicated sales contracts that demanded attention to minute details, those dreams of his wife were nothing except erotic soap operas. He had no patience with such nonsense, especially since his wife disclosed her dreams only vaguely, hampered by timidness that contained a certain amount of clumsiness. Her anxiety was fed by the knowledge that she erred from the image which the institution of marriage was holding up to her like a blind mirror. She was no longer able to recognize herself in it.

Besides, the bachelor's father was not interested in his wife's mind, but in her body. Imagination was situated across a chasm he rarely was inclined to leap. He understood symmetry yet the continents above and below logic were not for him. Even if he had tried hard, he was ill-suited to help her. His soul was not the garden she had hoped to find. Absent were the old rose trees whose branches had built a labyrinth of indestructible grace that grew toward the sky. And non-existent were brown stems whose thickness had lived through many winters.

As she found out during conjugal joys that were limited to her husband, his inner world resembled more an abandoned mining town where homes were shacks built in great haste. Even though during many moon nights she had wandered up and down the short, deserted main street like a forgotten mare and looked at every building, she saw only desolation. The one or two doors, still clinging crookedly to hinges which might have led her to rooms, she did not dare to push open. She was afraid she might find a dead woman in it, one of the many inamorati her husband had known before her. Contrary to the young wife whose carnal knowledge was marred as if she had barely escaped an ambush by Indian arrows, her husband had been an accomplished admirer of the female sex long before their matrimony. To make love was a simple, fulfilling act for him during which he easily climaxed. Orgasms were as necessary to him as the milk flowing from a mother's breast to suckle her new-born babe.

The bachelor's father could not help his wife out of her bearskin. He did not see her need because he had not been taught to sympathize with women. They were mysterious creatures to him whom he either feared or possessed. But always, including his mother, he considered women inferior to men. He was unable to see the clothes of spun silver his wife wore under her muteness and inhibition. What he noticed was enough for him. Her unusually pretty face and a well-made body in full bloom were perfectly capable of satisfying him. In his youthful cruelty he, like Aristippus some time before him, did not care that the fish complained as he was being eaten. His pleasure was not diminished by the pain he created. It rather was increased by it. The young woman did not know either how to overcome her husband's insensitivity. Nor was she aware of his well-concealed dependency upon her feminine intuition and her maternal instincts.

* * *

It must have started during the early part of their marriage in Ethiopia, this curious habit of hers not to open presents. Perhaps it had already begun during the evening of their wedding festivities, shortly after they had marched out of the small, octagonally shaped Armenian church in Addis Ababa. The bridegroom wore black with a white tie. His handsome head was encased by thick, luscious hair whose perfect hairline would serve him well in middle and old age when other men tended to become bald. The bride walked in white through the large crowd of wedding guests. Her sumptuous dress was crowned by two white roses from which a veil descended. It was almost long enough to conceal her slightly protruding stomach and the fact that she was seven months pregnant. Only those who knew her well noticed that her youthful, delicately colored face was now pale and there was a faint, trembling light in her eyes she did not have before.

One day early in their marriage the young woman became aware that she had developed the habit of not opening gifts any longer. Always delighted to get a finely wrapped parcel, she did not enjoy unfastening it. Instead she liked to place the box on top of her desk or a chest of drawers where she could see it and know the ribbon was uncut and its pretty bow untouched. Her husband was hurt that she did not want to know what he had brought her back from his long hours of work, the bleak tunnels he had to build in search for gold. He urged her to unclose his present, and to please him she tore its cover in great haste. But to his disappointment its content only evoked a quick thrill and then either was used with little joy or put in a drawer where it was soon forgotten. His wife had become afraid of the unknown. She who had loved to dive and to swim in her fast-moving river, these days preferred to remain on the surface, where she bobbed up and down between water and sky.

Her husband's imperceptiveness was connected with something that alarmed her. If he did not want to know what she thought, she became terrified at the idea of finding out what he felt. Perhaps there was nothing in the package! Perhaps all his assurances of love, his vows of fidelity were merely skin deep. In marrying her, in having children with her, was he not just following instinct and custom to which she as an individual was immaterial?

The longer she lived with her husband, the clearer it became that he did not know who she was, nor was he interested in finding out. She was his wife, one of his possessions, possibly his most valuable one. She could not be sure of even that. She no longer was certain of anything. She, who had just begun to unravel the threat that cocooned her soul, had dropped it. Now, instead of learning who she was, she walked in darkness. Blindly, she groped her way along back alleys. Their marriage contract had put a price tag on her. She now wore a label. She was easy to identify. Like her husband's traveling bags, she carried his name. She was his undisputed property.

The husband's life changed little after their marriage. He accepted with a certain ease the shallowness of life. For him the inescapable boredom of daily chores were not as hard to bear. He felt challenged by the swift cruelties of life that caught one unaware and made one feel trapped as if held by the claws of a huge cat. It was rare that he, ashen-faced, accepted defeat.

By contrast his wife was struck down by the emptiness of love and by a life so different from the one she had led before she wore her husband's ring. The glimpses she took at the interior worlds of her husband forced her to look at a void and she never regained the rosy hue of her cheeks. Within the form of him, where she had hoped to discover the sunken cathedrals of Debussy she had once seen below the waves, she found nothing except the green-blue waters of a bitter sea.

Naively, stupidly she had thought that love would turn man into Pantagruel, into a Gargantua whose mouth was big enough for her to take walks in, to discover fields among the molars farmers worked upon, and with pigeons fluttering above cusps and cavities. Where she had pictured a medieval Paris just around the corner of a canine tooth, she saw that her husband was only a gardener who grew cabbages. He in turn suspected she was insane to believe in giants, to accept a Thélème where stately Renaissance men and women were equally involved in the endeavors of Science and Art and where they enjoyed the pleasures of Love in endless, circular gardens.

The loss of the dream of love in exchange for a wedding band was a disaster for the young woman. Life no longer made sense to her. At night, when it was time to go to bed, when she knew she could not escape her husband's sexual demands, she prayed she were dead. Or at least old, with a thousand wrinkles clinging to her flesh to make her undesirable.

With dusk only a fast, faint silhouette against a dark East-

African sky, heralding a long night, she practiced a simulated death. Motionless, she lay on her back like an overturned beetle and tried to metamorphose her body into the stiffness of a board. She imagined worms nibbling at her. She attempted to think of the most disgusting odors, then wrapped herself up in them and hoped her husband would take notice. But he, entangled in his own pursuits, did not pay heed to her gloomy moods.

The more resistance the young woman offered, the quicker her husband went after her. It was the ancient game of Daphne and Apollo. Both were destined, without knowing it, to lose. Yet where the bachelor's father was conscious that he participated in old rites and roles and was quite content to play his part, his mother took their behavior seriously. She had not yet gained an aesthetic distance toward life but still, like a child, confused the mask with the real. She was unable to laugh at herself. She constantly attempted to fuse her dark, formless, rich subjectivity with an objective world whose rules she either did not understand or she rejected.

The young woman belonged to the tribe of Romantic heroes, the ones who roam huge, desolate landscapes and fall into their own pits while their eyes cling to the horizon. To avoid her destiny, she fled panic-stricken across stones, sand and roots only to trample upon her husband's heart that snapped shut around her ankle as if she had stepped into a rabbit trap. The pain of torn skin and muscles was almost unbearable and her head started to spin from loss of blood.

Sometimes in the afternoon she attempted to escape the oncoming night and the low-ceilinged bedroom where her husband demanded his marital rights with an audacity and with a savagery he would not have dared to use in a less isolated place where neighbors would have heard her screams.

* * *

One late, rainy afternoon when she could not overcome her depression, she quickly hugged her small children and lifted them out of the arms of their large-eyed Mamite, the young Ethiopian nursemaid. Then, not looking into the radiant eyes of her little daughter and ignoring the plaintive cry of her son who wanted to come with her, she jumped in

64

her car. Impatiently using her horn, she could hardly wait for the tall, tawny-necked, slowly moving Zabania, the gardener and night watch man, as he opened the wide, slightly vibrating tin gates that enclosed their compound. Barely aware where she was going, she raced at top speed along a broad, rain-glistening street that led to the center of the city. Somehow she got quickly through its noisy congestion where horse drawn buggies could be seen next to military jeeps the emperor used and old dirty, overcrowded buses that rumbled along while they swayed precariously from left to right. Then she took a road winding upward in endless, graceful curves with its borders lined by Eucalyptus trees that descended sharply into ravines.

She drove as far as the *Entoto*, one of the mountains that enclosed the city like a high entrance gate. Not long ago gallows had stood here and the winds had playfully turned the ghastly leftovers of a Shifta, an Ethiopian robber and murderer. It was the rainy season and she could hardly see anything through the windows of the car. The windshield wipers were unable, even at full force, to clear the windows of the onrushing waters.

Between the torrents outside and the tears running unchecked down her face, she was nearly blind. Pursued by the image of her husband and their tin-roofed house which she hated because she feared it would collapse from the weight of her heavy heart and the unceasing downpours, she kept to the outer edge of the steep, treacherous road. She hoped, since she did not have the courage to do so herself, something would hurtle her head-first into the narrow canyons, into nothingness. Yet this never happened . . .

In the evening she sat quietly facing her husband over their small meal in the dining room. Limply, she gave attention to him. After a while she reported some incidental household event that had occurred during the day. But she never heard what he said. I wish I were dead, she thought several times and looked at her husband without seeing him. After a while she began listening intently to a single voice that resembled a gurgling river. Nobody else seemed to notice the sound. It was a muted cry with a distinctly masculine timbre in the middle of its femininity. Within its center was a hard kernel, but the flesh around it was soft and sensuous. It was a murmur she had rarely heard before. Yet she recognized it instantly and knew she would hear it until she died. She understood that from now on she would measure love against this call.

The young woman was afraid of her husband. She knew he sensed something dark and spoiled in her. It was something that did not adhere to the *Madonna in the Rosegarden* ideal or to the mother of Christ who knelt down to her son. Least of all did it conform to the woman who humbled herself on front of man. Sometimes she reminded him of perfume in an old, fragile bottle. The odor, upon removal of the stopper, was intoxicating in its rich fragrance. But at the bottom of the frail glass a brown residue had gathered. If one tried to shake the flower-engraved, thin glass, the sediment rose slowly and mixed with the fluid. The eau de cologne then looked poisonous.

If the bachelor's father had known to softly knock at partially hidden doors and let his fingers trail delicately along the screen of summer windows so she would have had time to reach out from the inside and ever so lightly touch his fingertips, she would have been able to welcome him into her realm. But her husband had not been taught the art of gentle love-making. Where a glance or a silent bow to beauty would have sufficed, he with a strong kick of his boot, broke locked doors. In horror, she fled.

Words, whispered during the thin night hours when the veils of day become visible in the dark, would have helped where the act of love destroyed. Their physical clinging to each other was not enough to form a strong bond between them. It did not forge the mutual trust, the ropes flung from the back of one mountain to the next, so they could tie into a bridge across a steep ravine. As it was, husband and wife remained on their own sides. They never met. Only sparks of fire that the wind had carried through the air fused some parts of them, flickered for an instant, enough to reproduce, then died.

* * *

During their secret excursions at night she walked shackled in front of him. If she complained that the constant thrust of his hard knuckles hurt her back—since she never walked fast enough for him who pushed her—he put a collar around her neck and dragged her doglike.

The huge shades of their bed and curtains mingled with the fragrance of several trees. Their branches, usually proud and pointing heavenward now, as if agreeing with her mood, droopingly wound themselves around windowsills. Caught in fear and rage she lay on their hard bed. She dreaded his touch. Unable to speak to him about herself, she could not break the spell that bound her.

Fear of him prevented her from telling him about a still greater despair dwelling in her. She could not describe that formless, ugly mass which sometimes rose like a river around her and threatened to drown her. When she looked at his face hanging above her own like a dark sun, she recognized the features of the other man. It was the man whom she had met a hundred years ago while still a child in her father's house. Like a thief in haste who breaks the lock of a jewelry box, this man had handled her. Afterwards she always felt her cheeks were less rosy than those of other children.

While still small, she became angry and fearful of male adults who patted her head with big hands. They were unable to see that the creamy consistency of the child's skin was dotted with spots of sediment. The man, her father's best friend, had sworn the child to secrecy. The child kept the secret until it had festered within, then turned to stone. It became embedded within her flesh and grew, as if it were mutating into an organic substance, whenever her limbs started to stretch. It became her power and her curse.

At night, as she was pushed down by her husband on their bed and he invaded her most private thoughts, her river turned into fire. In it she saw the outlines of Siegfried. But he had become repulsive and was spurned by rage as he once more crossed the burning wall. With each step he took, with each thrust, she felt the stone within her. Sometimes the pain became so unbearable, she screamed with anguish. Her husband then thought she was delirious from pleasure. She could not explain what had happened. I wish I were dead, she thought again and wept.

Her flesh around the stone was smooth and rich. Her husband could not keep his hands off her. He never noticed that inside her, in the brown chambers of her soul and underneath the edges of the stone, there was the slippery flesh of a toad. After each copulation she was sick with grief and loathing. And she cried herself to sleep as she listened to her husband's light breathing.

* * *

During her most solitary moments in Ethiopia when misery pressed intolerably upon her and turned reality into human-sized boulders of ice, the young woman blew herself up until her toad's belly expanded and grew enormous so she no longer fitted into their living room, nor their house. She became oblivious of the exterior world. Even the voices of her children sank to the level of whispers carried away by the wind. Nauseated, she ran into the fenced-in garden. Once outside her home, she continued to grow rounder and fatter until she loomed above the town like a green-gray moon. She felt that by opening her mouth she would be able to swallow the city as it spread at her feet and eat its dotted lights littered among tree-studded hills.

At this point, having placed her sandals neatly at the edge of nowhere, she walked off her mountain and bent toward her feet around which the Red Sea lapped like an obedient dog. She laughed horribly when she saw the sea whom she knew in the form of a cat had changed into a canine. Revealing her teeth she squatted vulgarly with her legs fully exposed for the world to see what was meant for one pair of eyes only.

Later in the evening she and her husband sat down to their quiet supper for two. Their children were asleep in their room. A young, plump Ethiopian nursemaid lay stretched out on the carpet between their beds. Slowly chewing his food, the husband suddenly thought his wife was unusually pale. Instantly suspicious, he asked:

"What is the matter? What did you do today?"

She did not look at him when she said:

"Nothing. I took the children for a long walk."

But the heavy sullenness in her voice made him feel as if he were caught in a thick fog. Half blind, he was only able to see the constant blinking of a red light. After a short while the murkiness seemed to concentrate around his throat and chest. It was as if he were being suffocated. He coughed violently and brought up a morsel of bread. His wife watched him. Her eyes in whose coves he had swum during humid summer nights were now covered as if water lilies had grown there in too great abundance. Their long, snake-like stems moved through the opaque water searching for a prey.

When her husband forced her down upon their marriage bed, she knew he savored the residues of Brunhilde in her. The strong limbed myth floated through his mind in misty patches as he was caught in a net of dreams in which he saw himself as a hero. He did not know that the woman he kept against her will and whose forced body titillated him, wished he were dead. Even though he sensed that there was something wrong with his wife, he was not conscious that she hoped he were holding someone else captive—someone who was capable of enjoyng his ardor and violence. According to him, there were several such women. They all were madly in love with him, he said. Then why did he torment her?

Fearing the stabbing pain she had experienced before, she tried to distract herself by tracing his features that were held in space above her. She could escape as little from its rays as from the cruel desert sun that had drunk her blood. In the middle of their violent love play she was reminded of who he was.

Light-footed, she saw him run after the double-husked pig and the velvet-eyed gazelle that was as small as a hare. Its tiny, exquisitely shaped hooves looked as if a master had worked with onyx. Racing in a jeep through the open savannah he chased mercilessly the cheetah who competed with the swiftness of the wind. Without hesitation, he killed the Lesser Kudo for her comely horns. Long before others, his large eyes squinting in the sharp, vertical sun rays, he spotted the animals among the thorn-adorned bush of the immense East African landscape.

The soft gleam of his eyes whose lure she could not withstand drew her until she fell into them as if her foot had been caught among rhizomes. They caused her to stumble headlong into a concealed lake. The water was shallow. She quickly reached its muddy bottom writhing with leeches and snails. Slowly the blue-green cove turned black. Her gasping mouth and her dilated nostrils filled with slime and sea-weed. Entangled, she was taught once more the suffocating ugliness of death.

Her husband was a hunter, a warrior, trained in the loathsome art of war. Often he killed. Sure of his skill, his gun aimed with pride at heart and eyes. Before setting out to kill big game, he shot a rabbit just to bring good luck to the hunting party. He was proud of his expertise. Inside his head he carried a sun-parched desert where clocks stood still. Once man survived because he was a hunter. This memory was her husband's religion.

Of love he understood little. But he enjoyed sex and knew how to survive. A poet he was not. He did not know that gold was hidden in the bottom of his eyes. His eyes were sharp but his awareness of beauty in its timeless form was dim as if he could barely get glimpses through seven layers of a veil.

The feelings of the young woman toward her husband were not of a sensual nature. When she reached for him, which was almost never the case since it was he who pursued her in a pitiless manner, it was fear that curbed her finger tips, not desire. She needed his protection, and his muscles that were stronger than hers and his heavier bones.

At her right side he slept the light sleep of the hunter. At her left was the thin, sturdy cloth of the tent. Nothing except canvas separated them from the hyenas creeping outside under a full moon. Their laughter was muted. They were not comfortable with the closeness of healthy human scent in their nostrils. Hunchbacked they hobbled between the tight strings and poles of the tents. She could hear their breathing as well as her husband's. Pushed by hunger, they tried to reach the dead boars strung up in the trees.

During the evening most members of the safari had assembled around a quickly built fire. After supper, stories were swapped, jokes were told and considerable amounts of beer were drunk. The cans were hardly empty before they were snatched up by waiting Ethiopian villagers who sat quietly on their haunches at the periphery of the camp. The cook distributed the remains of the meal among thin, hungry children. For each morsel they received they bowed low and murmured shyly their thanks with downcast eyes. With a sharp knife the heavy pigs were swiftly disemboweled by the silent hunting guides whose emaciated arms belied their strength. After midnight when everyone had gone to sleep, the coagulated blood left between cavities, bones and skin was struck by moonlight. Silver and black melted obscenely with each other.

With her eyes wide open in the bright darkness of the moon that shone through the tent, the young woman lay on her back and listened with over exerted ears to the hyenas. She did not want to turn toward her right side where her husband slumbered. She did not even glance at her left for fear she would see again how the earth had opened—how Gaia had been torn by bombs that slew her to the entrails. Next to her was an abyss that seemed bottomless. Like Pascal she wanted to put a chair at its edge to prevent her fall. Quickly, so her husband would not know that she was awake and would not reach for her, she knitted her net. She kneaded the beads between her forefinger and thumb. Not the small, white pearls of her childhood, but the bigger ones, the ancient yellow beads she had seen in the palm of her Armenian father-in-law.

His old hand was fragile. The skin of his fingers had become thin from age and ceaseless work. On the back of his hand blue branches of veins mingled with brown dots. Attracted by the beauty that sprung from thumb and nervously fondled beads, she had wanted to know what he did.

"Calming my nerves," the frail Armenian had hastily answered in Italian, the language they conversed in. The old man's eyes were fading fast but as usual he cast a disapproving glance at her and closed his mouth tightly. Her pinkish-white lipstick and the red nail varnish she wore on her long nails classified her, his only son's wife and the mother of his grandchildren, as a prostitute.

Had he seen her as a bird of prey or as a Gypsy who danced and sang in a circus where her wide, dirty skirts swept across the sawdust, she could have understood this old man whose cultural concepts were so different from her own. But when he made a moral judgment, he hurt her. Why is he doing this? He has no idea who I am, she thought unhappily. The blunt knife her father-in-law used, tore her nerves and

71

opened the doors of hate within her. Some of their poisonous content poured out, soiled the air and, since her husband stood close by, was transferred to him as well.

Unknowingly or simply not caring, her father-in-law had distressed her several times. Never more so than when their daughter, after eighteen agonizing hours of labor and with the help of dangerous forceps, was borne. He, who had a year and a half earlier rushed to the hospital to see his minuscule, wrinkle-faced grandson, never came to visit his granddaughter.

"It's only a girl," said the delicate Armenian with his white hair that stood short and defiantly above his narrow forehead. And he stayed home. Only later when the toddler tried to pull herself up between his bony knees did he smile at his little granddaughter whose luminous, black eyes resembled his own to a large extent.

In agony the young woman knitted her net and spun her dreams that would hold her so she did not drop forever into blackness. She let herself be rolled up in her reveries, the net dragging her through the ocean and toward the waiting boat. When she came close to the ship that was clearly outlined against the horizon, she started to gasp.

While she was carried by the bitter transparent current, she tried not to look down. Once she had dared a glance. Afterward she had become so nauseated, she fainted. Had it not been for three wooden crosses, the ones she had seen as a child in a village churchyard, she, so she now believed, would not have awakened again.

From this night on, a night spent in Germany as a child, when heavy bombers cut the sky into half she understood why man had to believe in myths, legends and religions. The most marvelous invention of man was the idea of a savior, of a mysterious figure who suddenly stepped forward, had peeled off a stone wall when it was time to die. Christ was the symbol, implanted early within her, of a dead end street. At the last moment he raised his magic wand high into the air and the houses parted before the pursued. The buildings revealed a secret passage through which the hunted one could escape breathlessly. The deadly load of bombers, killing others by the thousands had let her live. Why? Before she stopped knitting, she always asked the same question. It was one of many riddles no one knew the answer.

The young woman's husband was born among the silent mountains of the legendary land of Prester John. They were holy mountains inhabited by monks, mountains forbidden to women, including female goats. The animals were not allowed to be hauled up in baskets to feed the monks who lived on top of sheer rocks. By contrast, male goats were always welcome to enrich a meager meal.

* * *

When the father of the bachelor had asked his wife, "What more do you want?" he implied that she was not satisfied with the material wealth with which he had surrounded her and their children. She was furious with him for having understood her so little. She realized he was working hard. She was keenly aware he did all of which he was capable to provide his family with a decent standard of living. And it upset her that he did not know who she was.

Money was not her goal. It was, of course, important. It was the golden calf men clung to after their ideal had vanished beyond a mountain top. Gold replaced the voice they had heard before. It blocked the rivers within them. Gold was the butterfly pierced to a board. It was a solidified dream—dead but visible. Whereas before the dream had been alive, floating like a jelly-fish, a blueish-translucent mermaid in a turquoise sea. Most of her life the young woman had been surrounded by family and friends who either had money or were in the process of accumulating it while she watched. She stood only inches away from the stream of gold of which she had no part.

In the early afternoons while the sun still stood almost in the zenith and her children took their nap after they were rocked to sleep by their patient nursemaid, the young woman sat in her cool living room and read. But soon she dropped her book and her thoughts reverted restlessly to her husband's words "what more do you want?"

She knew wealth would buy her time. It would provide her with an extraordinary carpet that lifted her gently above the sordidness of life. Long ago she had understood that floating above roof tops would render her visible against an evening sky. She saw herself as a golden, painted, human sized, wooden statue kept out of reach. This was one of her favorite dreams. After several years she reduced the size of the sculpture so it fitted into a glass bottle. The image which had once hung in the sky was now miniaturized so it could easily be stuffed into a dark pocket. There its content changed. Each time she stole a glance at her bottle, empty for others, she saw the face of a tiny water lily with her leaves folded like the wings of a caged bird. It was her, preserved for eternity. Or at least as long as the glass bottle did not break.

She also knew that ultimately she would not be able to escape money. Like Columbus, she would have to convert money into sails and into ships that moved through dreams of fear and guilt. Those wooden ships had been frail yet they were so strong that they were able to cross the border from a flat world into a round one.

To get hold of what she was looking for, she had been forced off her bewitched rug. She had seen herself fall through the sky and like Icarus had plunged head first into the sea. Only the tip of a wing had been momentarily visible. A poet had watched her disappear. He thought she was a ship, sunk forever. Yet one day someone saw her head and bony shoulders floating on the sea. She had survived.

It was the sea from which she had come. It was the sea she had to return to if she wanted to know who she was. She had to become one of the Japanese women who dive naked day after day to the bottom of the sea to search for pearls.

With her eyes wide open she sat on her red sofa on top of Ethiopia's magic mountains and saw herself with a cord slung around her waist. It was the only garment she wore. With it she plunged into the cold water. The lifeline was attached to a boat. The man in it was ready to pull her up when she ran out of breath and when her flesh quivered and the whiteness of her skin started to turn blue. The rope was the stem of the water lily along which she glided into the unknown. The heavy twine permitted her to dive deeply but it spot-bound her to the boat and the man who held the rope. Safety and responsibility no longer allowed her to roam freely even though now her forms were more refined than before. She had stripped off some of the fat that clung obstinately to her stomach and thighs. It was the roundness, the puppy fat of a young girl, her armor and her prison.

* * *

Long after she had cut herself loose from man and boat, had flown off the East African mountains and gotten a divorce in New York, the reader of the lie detector who had been asked to test her to see if she qualified for a job she wanted on Wall Street, was puzzled. Even though he searched thoroughly, he could not detect any falseness. Then he said he had never encountered anyone before who inhaled the way she did.

"You do not seem to breathe at all," he said quietly.

Since he did not ask her, she had not told him she was well acquainted with the bottom of boats as they slowly rocked above her. Nor did she mention that her lungs had expanded.

Money, she saw clearly, was important to survive. Money and power were the poles around which the world pivoted. Every day she watched how hard people worked to get it. How difficult it was for most men and women to earn their daily bread, and how easy for a few to gather large heaps of gold. Money was the most slippery of all substances. Like quicksilver it rolled here and there. Now one saw it, now one did not. There was apparently no law to control it. This appealed to her. Fortuna, bound in smooth marble, was still blindfolded even though she appeared to favor those players who had already assembled a small stack of silver and gold in front of them.

* * *

When the bachelor's father had asked his mother:

"What more do you want?" he had put the "wanting more" strictly within the context of money. He could not have been more wrong. He could not have forced her out of her chimeras faster, plucking her from his sky.

It was not money or power by which she was driven. Her wishful thinking was as unconnected with reality as the elaborate dreams of the builder of an empire.

75

Unlike her husband she understood that Alexander, long before he and his Macedonians reached Babylon, had seen the city with the eyes of his soul. The fierce, young warrior who lived on a horse's back had, so she strongly felt, the genius of a poet. In his youth his mind was nurtured by Aristotle where—crossing centuries—logic already seemed to mingle with a Kantian a priori thinking and where the imagination ruled. His thoughts gave form to ideas that drifted upon air, rose out of a void, out of black nothingness and solidified into new Greek worlds. She saw Alexander like she saw Baudelaire, who had picked up the dirt of Paris and turned it into gold.

The young woman knew Alexander had seen Babylon with the eye of his mind years before adventurous merchants and marauders had first reported her wealth and beauty. Babylon was the burning border of his empire. The city was the illusive line between earth and sky that pushed him mercilessly onward. Young, barely in his mid-twenties, Alexander forged his empire with brutal force and skill. A mortal, he could not, as his mythical forefathers had been able to, cross the gulf that separated him from his ideal without applying his foot soldiers and mounted men. And he went nowhere without taking with him his slaves, concubines and minions. One of his male lovers was a bewitching boy from Persia. Alexander preferred him to his wife, a princess he had quickly married to assure him an heir.

Unable to sleep and tossing about, she watched as his wagons were pulled by slow oxen. On muddy roads the heavy vehicles were pushed by his soldiers, weak from diseases. Then there were his horses. Swift, splendid and unafraid to cross wild rivers, they cantered past burning villages and towns. They did not seem to smell the stench of decaying flesh.

It was this horseback bred freedom, the warrior's scope, the young woman craved. Yet even more, she coveted a liberty that was no longer earthbound. Even Alexander's fast horses, whose hooves barely touched the ground upon which they galloped, were not enough for her. Besides she felt that Alexander and her husband had too much in common. She desired an unlimited, rootless autonomy that allows one to float in space . . . the dangerous abandonment of Hölderlin.

She felt at home in the poet's world built from water, fire and air. She wanted to be part of his universe that excluded the earth. Her ideal was his unbound privilege that ended in madness and in nothingness. Hölderlin became a speck of dust in the sky where it span forever, dancing, turning until the eye could no longer see it.

At night, lying on their wide bed, she would have liked to but dared not to shout from the top of their thin roof, "I would like to be a balloon!" like the one that had come off a child's hot wrist around which it had been fastened. It was, of course, impossible to describe this wish to her husband. He would not have understood her. He would only have become more alarmed about her childish longings and about her mad ideas that had started to threaten him like a contagious disease. Husband and wife were separated by centuries that stretched sometimes beyond human memory. The sea between them was too wide, too treacherous. One of them would surely drown.

* * *

The bachelor's father knew only the wilderness of Africa into which he had been born during a rain-drenched night in the beginning of September, the commencement of spring in East Africa. He was at home in the Great Rift Valley that connects two terrible Ethiopian deserts, the Danakil in the north and the Ogaden in the south. He still walked along a deep gorge, carried by one of the loftiest landscapes little known to the rest of the world. These mountains were as hidden away, as inaccessible as Tibet and the Andean highlands.

From below, the bachelor's mother saw his father silhouetted way above her as he challenged the setting sun. Motionless, he stood on black rocks. His eyes did not flicker while he was surrounded by Ras Dashan in the northwest and Gojjam in the northeast. Fifteen thousand feet of rocks piled upon rocks. It was here where Queen of Sheba gave birth to Solomon's first son. She and her large-eyed child can be seen on the wall paintings of some of the eleven underground rock churches in Lalibela. Built in the early 13th century by King Lalibela, the churches were carved entirely out of rocks.

77

Embedded among high mountains Lalibela becomes shrouded in mist and inaccessible when the *big rains* fall. Not many have seen those shrines of early Christianity.

This was the country where Mentwab, the Beautiful, had ruled during the early 18th century. In Kusquam, south of Gondar, traces of her summer palace can still be seen. The branches of a wild fig-tree that grows outside of her former residence have caught the last breath of dying men, shiftas who were hung there. The castle is now almost completely ruined but the legend lives.

After the death of her husband, King Bacuffa, Mentwab, the light skinned queen, took over the power until her son, King Jesus II, was strong enough to reign. King Bacuffa was the one whose nose had been partly cut off because he had attempted to escape from Wahni, the Prison Mountain of the Princes. Had it been known that the king was dead Mentwab, a woman and her child, would have been overpowered by one of the princes from Wahni. Wahni, the inaccessible prison, often held close to a hundred princes. Perched like an eagle's nest on a mountain top, sheer walls dropped away into nothingness. Trying to break away from there usually meant certain death.

* * *

The young woman's husband, a hunter, understood only that Army boots protected him from snake bites. He could not accept that his wife craved high-heeled shoes. Those softly leathered things held by bows and rhinestones meant nothing to him. He disdained a foot inside a delicate slipper and did not want to know about toes and heels and the rest of Bi-pedal man's complex locomotion. To him it seemed the foot dressed in those fragile shoes became something else, just like Mercury's feet look different because of the wings attached to his Achilles tendons. The bachelor's father did not appreciate such types of metamorphoses.

In contrast, the young woman sometimes thought her husband still lived during an age when the horse, who now walks on its toes like a ballet dancer, still moved flat-footed. This ancestor of the horse was different from the current one. She, who adored the horse's indescribable grace, did not

78

picture one without seeing it rear upon his hind legs. And she imagined her horse as just having thrown off its rider, who now cursed and struggled among straw and dirt. Her stallion was free, unconquered by man. Occasionally, depending upon what time of day it was, her horse suddenly appeared with a long ivory horn protruding from his forehead. Amidst his mane, silky to her fingers, she could see the glimmer of a topaz and emerald. If she got quite close, she noticed the many-faceted reflection of a woman's face on the surface of the precious stones.

The young woman's horse had nothing in common with those four-legged creatures her husband knew how to ride bareback. As a child, he had become familiar with the small, sturdy Galla horses, as stubborn and hard-working as mules.

One night when he was in a good mood, her husband had told her about this tribe. Large-eyed she had listened to his tale. She was thrilled to hear that in the mid sixteenth century after the final defeat of the Somali by the Ethiopians, the fierce Gallas had crossed the border of Kenya and ridden into a horseless, war-weakened Abyssinia. Because of their horses, their round leather shields and the blond lion manes they wore as fear inspiring headgear, the Gallas quickly conquered huge spaces of land and became the largest tribe of Ethiopia.

There were special moments, usually during the short-lived dusk and dawn of Africa when the bachelor's father seemed to have inherited some of the ancient, aggressive spirit of the Galla warrior. Deeply sunburned, a color his mother detested because she considered Ethiopians inferior to Armenians, his face then shone darkly and his eyebrows more than ever had the shape of raven wings. Its black feathers had carried the young woman off the ground. Then the wings had broken and she had fallen head first into the bitter water of the sea.

V

Les clous dans notre poitrine, . . .
René Char
(Nails in our chest, . . .)

The revelation that she could not marry her Princeton man either, came unexpectedly for the bachelor's mother. It was the third August after her divorce. A pale-yellow sun stood upright in the morning sky. The air was cold as if autumn had already deposited its heaps of perishable gold. Yet the lawns outside the windows of the car were green and crisp. Slowly, constantly pulling up steep hills and gliding down upon their backs, mother, children and their grandparents moved through the magic world of the Rocky Mountains. These were mountains that suddenly hiccuped and spit stones. One of them broke the front window of the car.

The German grandparents of the two small siblings had arrived by boat. They brought their car for an extensive cross-country trip through the United States and parts of Canada. The distorted French of Montreal caused them surprise mixed with pleasure that arose from their contact with friendly citizens. In the south they met with the long, arid stretches of the Mexican landscape only interrupted by a sombrero protected farmer and his dusty donkey. As they watched him walking slowly into the blue dusk, man and beast became imprinted upon an immense sky and the earth.

During a hot May afternoon the grandparent's vessel had docked in Newark. Later the bachelor remembered how young his grandfather looked as he leaned across the railing of the ship. Wide-shouldered and lean, he wore a light summer suit and a straw hat on his semi-bald head. Waiting for customs to come on board, he had time to leisurely observe his grandson.

They boy had grown again and promised to be tall. Now nine years old, he had inherited the heavy German bones where each limb was in symmetry to the spine. His muscles and tendons were covered by flawless flesh and skin. He had partly inherited his mother's prominent zygomatic arches and his cheeks caught the light in a soft glow. It looked as if the child had been fed on milk and flowers. In years to come, as a young adult, his cheeks would cave in. The child's roundness would be taken off his face. Strength would be added to beauty.

Several weeks prior to the boy's departure for the Rocky Mountains, his grandparents had left New York and driven west. Then, in early August, the boy, his little sister and mother took a plane and joined his grandparents. Their small aircraft out of Denver had flown quite low across velvet-green plains, lit up by the slanting rays of a setting sun. Beneath the twin-engine the land undulated in an unending, green dance. "Look how beautiful it is," the young woman said to her children who were starting to get fidgety. She loved nature and wanted to develop her son's and daughter's aesthetic sense. Unable to instruct them about religion because she did not believe in the teachings of the Church, she wanted to replace a dogmatic institution with other spiritual values.

After they landed in Colorado, the young woman, her parents and her children moved by car for three weeks from south to north through the Rocky Mountains. They started in Mesa Verde where they climbed the high, steep ladders that led to the abandoned villages of the cliff dwellers. On their precarious ascent the children's sandaled feet were above the young woman's hands and head. Squinting into the sun, she watched with fear as her daughter's small, brown legs moved skyward. Without halting once the child pushed herself upward and was unafraid of the considerable height it reached finally. Then she stood defiantly at the ledge of the cliff and looked down into the deep gorge below her.

With the help of some broken pottery and a young, enthused guide they tried to imagine what life must have been like long ago in the waterless airy caves where one wrong step would throw one into a stony depth. Mothers must have tied their offspring for several years to their backs, hips or stomachs. And each thunderstorm was like the last Day of Judgment.

Their journey ended in Jackson Hole, Wyoming.

Before they got there, every day revealed new surprises. There were a few turbulent times at breakfast because grandfather and mother disagreed about children's table manners.

The grandfather had tried to push his own children to peaks they could not cling to but pitifully slid off on their behinds the moment they got there. Shame burned the skin of their hands as they tried to slow down their fast descent. Good behavior at table were one of grandfather's ideals, he now tried to impose on his grandchildren too. But the young woman whose conduct at table was impeccable, remembered too vividly the pain with which those flawless bearings had been purchased. She preferred her children to be less perfect. Especially while they were sitting outdoors at a roughly hewn wooden table and benches, besieged by paper plates, plastic knives and half broken spoons. At first rather patiently she tried to explain her point of view to her father. He was not easy to convince and considered his values superior to those of his daughter.

"That may be, but they are my kids and we are on vacation. I want them to enjoy this trip. It is the wrong place and time for table manners."

The young woman said quickly with a red face after her father's long explanation. A moment later she was surprised and a little frightened that she had dared to defy him. But had she not acted impulsively, she would have never had the courage to oppose her father.

"You are just like your mother," her father threw abruptly at her, his eyes flashing angrily. The young woman got up and left the table. She knew if she had answered her father, they would have gotten into an ugly argument. After a harrowing divorce her father had remarried. The boy's maternal grandmother was a forbidden subject. It was only used in moments of great anguish.

There were days when one mountainous wonder after

wonder rose like the skilled voice of a singer overcoming four octaves until it ends in unaccustomed splendor. The dimensions of the West were such that Europe seemed more like a garden in comparison. Had it not been for the limitless space of Africa, the young woman would have been ill-prepared for this type of jagged beauty. Its width and depth stood in sharp contrast to New York which specializes in narrow, man-made canyons.

She had heard and read about the canyons. She had seen slides of them, had attended lectures given by geologists, anthropologists, paleontologists, ecologists and had listened to just plain worshipers of nature. Yet when she actually confronted the Grand Canyon, it was not what she had been told and shown. After their first glance at the Canyon that extended one mile below them so the earth looked as if it had been torn apart, she started to understand what American myths were made of.

This was no longer just dry earth and a cold distant sky above it as she knew it while she passed the Empire State Building or the World Trade Center. Or as she walked hastily across the slightly hilly and crooked pathways of Wall Street to which odors and the sounds of Europe still cling persistently.

She felt that the earth of the Grand Canyon and the sky above it strongly resembled Gaia and Uranus caught in an unmentionable moment of intimacy. Her blood rose to her face while, indecent like a voyeur, she looked at the mile-wide opening of the Canyon. Observing the gorge, she imagined that she had stumbled upon a woman who had just been thrown to the ground, and eagle spread, was fully exposing her hidden features.

Then, to calm herself, she thought that if the Abyssianian abyss had given birth to a bloodline of two thousand years, there was no telling what this Canyon might do. She wished she had listened longer to the Native Americans. She would have loved to have learned the language of their dances. Secrets of the past and the future appeared to be hidden in their rhythmic movements. Like the bee, the Native American spoke with his body.

* * *

When the bachelor's family arrived in Wyoming, they were joined by the mother's third potential marriage candidate. Her Princeton man had also flown in from the east. They had just picked him up at his hotel. After a short stroll on the wooden sidewalks of Jackson Hole, where one could barely avoid colliding with cowboys whose endless, elegant legs had grown on three steaks a day, they were headed for the white sulphur springs of Yellowstone Park.

As always, the young woman enjoyed looking at her beau's facial features. She liked the way his tongue pushed through healthy front teeth and just barely touched his full lips before they formed the sound of the "th." Her mother tongue did not possess those two letters in this phonetic combination. A "th" was pronounced simply as a "t," dragging the "h" silently along like a disobedient puppy. She had to learn the "th" during long lessons.

Those tedious English sessions were given by an elderly gymnasium teacher who, in order to be more explicit, forced her tongue way beyond upper and lower lips. To her ten-year-old students, the well meaning spinster looked ludicrous, if not loathsome. It was like watching a short, reddish snake probing with a wide tongue into slimy corners. Her tongue tried to find hidden toads and the invisible egos of her students. Only later, after the young woman noticed that the modern Greeks, the descendants of her lost heroes, also used the "th," did she become reconciled with it. But for a long time she had feared the teacher's tongue as if it had been capable of exploring unknown cavities of hers, dragging forth the ugly secret of which she was ashamed.

She remembered again when she was a child, a stone had been implanted within her. It had been forced upon her while she was fully conscious, as if she had been a caught fugitive and burned with a hot iron where it hurt her the most. So far she had been able to conceal this mark under her clothes. Also, by now it was partly covered with secretion and deeply embedded among mucous membranes. Tendons, blood and muscles protected it as if it were the bed of an oyster destined to grow a pearl. But she felt as if the spinster's tongue tried to expose it. It was as if her tongue while

84

forming the "th," attempted to pull off her dress so she would have to stand naked in front of her class, pitilessly exposed to forty pairs of hostile eyes. They were staring, cold eyes that had been assembled in a large classroom. The room looked like a prison because its windows were built too high within an impenetrable wall.

No, the "th" had not come easily to her. It was only after she met Homer in the disguise of Racine, and when she fell in love with a seventeen centuries old Hector and Adromaque who now spoke the French of Versailles, that she was able to see beauty in the "th." It was Medea moving at night in the shade of Athens' Acropolis who convinced her that the "th" had its value. And it was Jason standing on a stone stage under a glittering moon that coquettishly danced among full-skirted clouds who helped her. She needed the myth to grasp reality.

* * *

It must have been close to noontime. They still had a while to drive before they would have lunch. The Princeton man's stomach had started to send out gurgling signals of distress. To appease his hunger, he opened a can of beer. There was only a slight hiss as if a snake had been stepped upon as he bent back the metal opening of the can. Quickly, the yellow-golden liquid, a competitor of the sun that now hung almost straight above them, poured forth. But her father, who was driving, had heard the sound. Disturbed, he gave the Princeton man a disapproving look. One of the rules in her father's silver book of etiquette that included faultless table manners even when seated on timber benches in a picnic area miles away from civilization, stated clearly: "No intoxicating beverage before sunset. Anyone who drinks before evening is an alcoholic." Her father stubbornly believed that. Innocently her beau had broken this paternal commandment. And she trembled with fear.

She had been indoctrined by her father's dictates, with no pains spared. She learned that even if one had not adhered to a regulation because one did not know it existed, it entailed punishment. Her father castigated not out of vindictiveness, but out of respect for statutes. With no visible passion, he had applied the whip. The principles he obeyed were his garden fence. It enclosed his entire property. The barrier was made of thin wire and hardly visible night or day. Invariably, the rampart caught even the smallest intruder whose steps caused an alarm to be set off. The noise woke the hunting hounds of her father who furiously chased the stranger and usually caught him.

Since the Princeton man resembled her father, both physically and in his emotional constitution, the young woman had been hopeful but also apprehensive about their encounter. She understood it would take only a small incident to tip the fragile scale one way or the other. The opening of the beer can before lunch had upset the balance. It caused the scale to go down, when just as easily it could have gone up.

The young woman turned pale. She knew she would have to send her lover away. She was too weak and insecure and still too much her father's daughter to resist most of his fears and desires. She had not yet broken the umbilical cord, even though she herself had given birth to two children. It seemed her father was forever the pearl fisher in the boat out of whose shadow her husband had sprung. She realized now that both men had taken turns holding the rope slung around her waist while she dove below them. As she roamed the deep and searched for oysters, she thought she had been free. It was a freedom bought by enlarging her lungs so they could hold air longer than other lungs. Now, while the rope tightened around her waist, she knew she needed more than skills and more than daily practice in swimming and breathing in order to gain independence. She shivered with despair and cold. Without the cord and the boat above her how would she be able to get back to the surface? Or would the huge ocean keep her a prisoner too? Would the sea send her its messengers that shot silently out of nowhere? She was terrified of the sharks who might bite into her flesh with their acicular, razor-sharp teeth that grow back each time one of them gets broken off. Those sea monsters might nibble at her legs, her arms, as if her limbs were but an appetizer, a bun of fresh bread one crumbles between fingers and thumbs while one waits for dinner.

What she could not comprehend was her father's

acceptance of her husband, so unlike him, while he refused the Princeton man who resembled him in many ways. After she had taken her children, who still wore diapers, and fled from her husband's East African house back home to Germany, her father, at the slightest sign of repossession from her husband, had handed her back to him like a caught convict. As soon as her husband had followed her, the escaped prisoner, her father weakened and she had submitted to both men. Now, years later, when she was almost sure she could come to love someone like the Princeton man, her father rejected her choice. Why? Was his fear of alcoholism that strong? Or were there other revulsions and desires involved he did not dare to put into words?

Her father had liked her husband's quick, practical mind that was straight and narrow like a man-built canal. But he apprehended and admired the Princeton man's fluid thoughts, his slight tendency toward mysticism, his articulate delight in beauty, his indulgence in drink and his refusal of reality and mediocrity. Her father was afraid of the unmeasurable river. He understood her husband's simplicity, his drive that had quickly produced two children, his capacity to focus upon one subject with endurance, if not obstinancy. And her husband's explicit maleness, his body that did not contain any opening where even a trace of femininity could hide, had caught her father almost as strongly as it had enticed her.

What her father did not grasp was her otherness from him and her childlike elusiveness which she could only express in negative terms, in the sensation of having been caught and of being forced to walk in front of her husband with her hands tied to her back. Her father was the man she had loved the longest, but he was a man, not a woman like herself. He did not speak her language. He lived on the other shore. The one she could not reach.

Her father did not know and he could not see her being restricted to sit upon a rock that was placed a little higher than other rocks so her husband could watch her and could use her as a focal point while he chased gazelles and wild boars in the vast Ethiopian savannah.

Her father, who lived on the other side of the mountain, could not see she was nightly force-fed by her husband.

* * *

Long ago as a child in Germany she had once watched a middle-aged peasant woman stuff a goose. With her knees spread wide, the woman had sat on a three legged milking stool. Her red face was framed by a black kerchief and her lips were pressed tightly together. Between her legs that were covered by a long, gray skirt, she held a fat goose. The neck of the bird was stiff with food that had been stuffed into its throat. With one hand the farmer's wife held its beak wide open. And with the forefinger and thumb of her other hand she pushed, what looked like a thick porridge, behind the tongue of the goose. Forcefully, she slid it across its tiny, red vestiges of teeth. The goose screamed wretchedly and choked. It tried to cough, to hiss, to vomit. It struggled to free its wings from two fleshy knees and two ugly thighs that pressed its lungs together. But the woman held the bird firmly. Cruelly, she closed its beak until the bird had swallowed again and again. Its white feathers that had shone in the sun while it swam proudly in the village brook, were soiled with cooked grain. And its downy plumage on its stomach, so fluffy and lovely to touch, was glued together with dust and slimy dark-green excrement.

* * *

At times, when her marriage had been caught like a boat in terrifying whirlpools, she felt like that goose. For many years at breakfast, the smell of porridge, loved by her father and husband, nauseated her.

Who was her father whose face was so familiar since she had been a child? Who was he of whom she saw now only fractions in the mirror of the car as he drove them through Wyoming's mountains? Who was her father and the grandfather of her children, the man whose strong, well shaped hands held firmly the steering wheel of his car?

They were in the middle of a spectacular mountain world. Mountains that whistled and blew small brown children off the road as if they had been giggling leaves. They were mountains that ate a busload full of tourists for a snack. These were the mountains whose hair had been singed by Indian fires. Their furious flames had caused bald patches.

88

Day after day they drove through the Rocky Mountains whose fur along their flanks had been pulled in large fistfuls by white settlers, by man in his unending need for space and for new territory. To the children's mother these mountains were so different from the benevolent, old hills of Germany.

They were not the gentle mountains of her childhood that curved next to the lazily flowing *Neckar* and next to the castle of Heidelberg destroyed by Tully during the Thirty Year War. Castle, bridges, churches, men with their wives and children, their horses and dogs, all had been like grain between two millstones. Between the Catholic field marshal who first replaced Wallenstein's army and then Napoleon's fighting forces, Southern Germany had suffered greatly. Not only the Catholic army, but the Protestant and French armies as well caused almost total destruction. Land, people and their possessions vanished as if they had never existed.

At first the enemy had not been sure if the towns and villages he invaded had packs of bloodhounds who would lurch themselves at the intruder's throats. But after a while when the soldiers realized that most doors had broken locks, they gained confidence. Dragon-like, the enemy armies prowled through the manyfold dukedoms of Bavaria, Würtemberg and Saxony, vestiges of the Holy Roman Empire. Eating off the land, the dragon's head spat fire, its teeth sank into soft flesh, and its tail dragged through black soot. Red trails of blood crisscrossed the land, bodies of men, women and children were cut open, hung upon trees, upside down, as if they were dead pigs. War, the great hunter, reverted man into an ape again. Mad, it chased him relentlessly through towns, villages, plowed fields and forests.

More than two centuries later, the bachelor's mother walked with her father among the same forested hills. Both of them looked across the river and their eyes caressed the ridge and ruins of the great castle, burned by Tully and never rebuilt. At their leisure, they moved in and out of sun and shade and she listened to her father's voice. His was a voice that did not sing in church. Instead it spoke in whispers among trees. He, whose roar had terrified her many times during childhood, now told her riddles and rhymes.

It was almost as if Grandmother held her again while the

child hid her head amidst her soft, large bosom. When she was little, Grandmother's arms had embraced her so she no longer heard the heavy bombers that flew above them. Slowly the planes had dropped their deadly loads. No god paid attention to children's hands folded in prayer. The child learned early that there was no kindhearted god. The only god she knew was cross-eyed from abhorrence. Burned, shriveled-up and almost dead he clung to a fiery church wall which the next detonation would destroy.

Stimulated by the silence around them and by the fresh scent of pines and mushrooms, father and daughter felt nature playing her old tricks again. The earth became highly visible in her perfumed dress. When bending down, one could touch her flower-embroidered substance. The young woman watched her father's lips. Words rolled off them in an inspired sequence, only an inch short from incantations. If his voice had been a fraction higher and if there had been a gram of alto in it, it would have been a woman's. It could have been Grandmother's.

Her father was brought up as a Catholic. Yet she never saw him kneel in front of an altar. But now he walked next to her as if he wore the glowing, white robe of a priest. Until this day she had not known how much he loved the soil he stepped upon. He worshiped the trees that had grown again after man, the war-maker, had burned them down. Man, the hunter, had set a forest on fire so each pine trunk became a burning candle. Man, the killer, enjoyed watching a cathedral burn. Man, the ruthless adult, did not care that fire licked the sky, swept away a child's dream, its trust in grown men and women and its faith in a benevolent god.

She knew, as she walked through spring next to her tall father, she had become intoxicated with fresh air and had lost her balance among the trees. She no longer saw the grudges she bore him. Now the young girl did not remember the cruelties they had flung into each others faces. For many winters they had thrown snowballs at each other in whose midst lay a stone. The father's recollections about his anxieties over his daughter, the rebellious adolescent, were receding fast. And in the young girl's mind vanished all images of her father's jealousy, his coercing her into assuming the unwanted role of wife and mother. She even forgot the mask that had been cruelly put upon her head by his name.

The young girl had hated the family's name which did not allow her to find her own identity. She was only known as a member of her father's family and not for her own sake. Hiking through the German forest, close to her father, she did not remember her struggle to pull off the disguise. She had overcome her screams of revolt against her father and her hatred of him who kept her bound to the boat when she wanted to be free. And she no longer recalled that her father who was utterly unhappy in his own marriage, had not rested until she chose a husband of her own, his surrogate.

She had been disgusted with her father because, with her eyes not yet experienced enough to see in the dark, she thought he held up the finely chiseled chalice filled with wine only for her, while she watched him bend down and lap water like a dog. She could not accept that one moment she saw her father's face filled with light, while the sky was reflected in his eyes and the sun pulled playfully at his high forehead. Then the next instant, as she had turned her back and blinked her eye a split second, she was startled to see him stand in a dark corner urinating noisily. Too young, her wings too short and stubby, she could not reconcile the god and the ape. It was natural for other men to fornicate. But when it came to her father, she wished that the ape who lived from the waist down, could be turned into stone. Only after she had finally become a fully grown woman was she able to see her father was not two men, separated in the middle, but one being whose scope was tremendous.

Giantlike, her father's feet were able to walk across broken glass without cutting himself, while his head appeared to touch upon low hanging clouds. So tall was he that his face, moonlike, seemed to loom above the tree tops. The daughter who walked next to him, saw only his feet and his handsome, balding head with its mouthful of healthy teeth. His body in between was hidden by the odorous pine trees among which they moved for a long time. The young girl would be a middle-aged woman before she was able to comprehend who her father was. Only then did she see him as a man of normal proportions.

Half of her life the young woman was thrown from one

shore to the other. The ape constantly interfered with the god. Until she reached maturity she felt as if she had been nothing except pieces of flesh tossed upon the surface of the sea. A leg of hers floated here, an arm over there. Torn apart, as if sharks had bitten into her, she had not lived as a whole being, but in shreds and as dead weight. Only a few vital parts of her had survived. She did not know that human beings could live as piecemeal and as fragmented splinters blown away by wind and waves. Only after she had finally assembled all of herself, did she realize into how many parts she had been broken, and how profusely she had bled. Now it seemed such a miracle to be alive, to walk upon the earth and to be aware of her limbs that fitted like a well-sewn dress. Then one windy morning she realized that she was no longer tied to the boat. She had left the sea.

When she was barely a juvenile, her father had split her apart. It had hurt so much that she often wished he had not returned from Russia where he had spent four years during World War Two. Cruelly, he almost severed the thin, invisible threads that held her together like cat guts. Mother had born her as a compact, tiny being. At birth she had been perfect in her form. Her soul had been in harmony with its body. She could not distinguish one from the other. With mother, life was simple. There was a deep, blind love between them. It was the inseparable bond that exists between mammals raising their young. Mother had borne her as a minute, downy creature. Incapable of speaking, she could only cry and howl. But she knew that Mother loved her. As an infant she had slept a lot and then as a toddler and child she had bustled back and forth happily, filling her stomach without thought. It was only when she matured and grew into something else that her problems started. Then Father, while she became an adolescent, destroyed her tidy, fluffy image of Eden. Mercilessly, he took a broom and swept her out of paradise, which as one knows, once outside remains inaccessible.

Into the water her father had thrown her like a Venetian housewife who tosses vermin into one of the busy canals. Glittering like the roof top of the dome across from the Gritti Palace, he sat in the evening sun. His beauty rivaled with that of Kubla Khan's abode. In her nostalgic longing she

92

suddenly forgot how afraid she had been of him and the great cats. Her eyes and her soul of which she was now acutely aware, only saw the splendid shapes across the tamed sea that was filled with black gondolas. Like elaborate coffins they floated along sixteenth century mansions that glowed with lights. Her body, spacebound, could not follow her visions. The yearning and the stretching of innumerable steel bands to their utmost limit, constantly threatened to snap her into two. If the hard strings had broken, she would have fallen into the water and disappeared. Sunk to a slimy bottom she would have been buried at the waterlogged foot of a palace. Or the cats would have gotten her. Yet she did not snap. To her utter amazement the stretching made her grow instead.

During the slowly moving years of pubescence she had observed her father as he briskly stepped along German city streets while he pointed out buildings in a particular style. Or he drew her attention towards wooden and marble statues into whose forms his words seemed to breathe life. Their white stone lips started to speak and their smooth, cold arms, that normally embraced a dead lover, suddenly appeared to want to hold her too.

Now, almost grown-up, their walk among the hills and forest of Heidelberg was something special. Her father was usually too introverted and too harassed by worldly obligations to speak to her with leisure. But that day the silent trees touched upon hidden layers within him. Their long branches reached beneath the patina. Twigs held by his fingertips that were made sensitive by their synaptic nerve endings, seemed to transfer some of their odor under his skin and into his bloodstream. His head started to feel light and he lost some control over his locomotion. Like a sailor just home from a long sea voyage, her father's legs embraced the pine needle covered ground in large, rolling motor movements. His speech for once had slowed down. There was no haste in his words and the silence between his sentences was drawn out like the lazy yawn of a cat. His nervous awareness of time which made talking to him difficult, was now absent. He had fully absorbed some of the peaceful environment that protected him like a glass telephone booth at the corner of a turbulent city street.

93

During their walk among the hilly paths of the *Philosophenweg* in Heidelberg from where they could see the castle across the river, her father had for the first time, and rather against his will, treated her as an equal. Instead of sending her to her room as in the past, he had asked her to come into his study. He had finally and rather reluctantly, allowed her to occupy a seat in the living room that was reserved for adults and special occasions only. During that long walk he had untied her from the boat on the sea and set her free.

After their extended hike they walked over the bridge to the other side of the river where the castle was. As if he had been the owner of the château, he showed her room after room of the magnificent building. Not as it was now, mostly in heavy ruins, but as it once had been before its destruction. In a dreamlike state she walked up and down wooden and marble staircases. Her new freedom permitted her to see different perspectives and angles of several familiar rooms. Space, she thought had been endless and huge like a cathedral, had shrunk into large living rooms. Where she had imagined that she had walked outside the building in the garden, she now discovered that the flowers she touched were piles of books upon which she had scurried back and forth. The books belonged to the library of her father. During many years he had collected and categorized the various texts which he considered his most valuable belongings.

While still a child, she had lived among her father's books. Before she was able to read them, she had sniffed at their cloth and leather bindings and had become intoxicated from their odor.

* * *

For hours that beautiful spring day the daughter walked with her father through the castle of Heidelberg. Reflected upon its high ceilings were the faint outlines of sun rays. When they came to the end of a narrow hallway on the ground level a strong odor rose from musty, urine-soaked walls. The parapets from where the repulsive smell came were hewn into the stony ground of the mountain. They were part of a basement that was forever solidified with the rocks into which it had been built.

Slowly father and daughter followed the obnoxious odor that grew fainter as it led them to an enormous wine cellar. Like huge, wooden eggs, hundreds of wine barrels were stored within high, dark vaults. Solid bedrock walls encased them. Then her father led her to a particular cask. It was so immense that on top of it a small dance floor had been built. Her father told her how in the past as soon as it got dark, ladies in white powdered perukes and long gowns with fresh roses pinned to their bosoms climbed the sturdy ladder, gallantly held by their escorts in silk and velvet tights. Until the early morning hours they danced on top of two thousand liters of wine. As she stood beneath the enormous barrel and its empty dance floor, the young girl heard clearly the throaty laughter of women and men.

Then she suddenly remembered that as a child she had once listened to their voices. But they had been too far away. She heard them only after they had wound themselves through long, dark hallways. The voices had come to her as if carried on a faint stream of music. By the time they reached her ear, cocked in the dark against her slightly opened door, the only light in a black sea, the sounds were reduced to those of humming bees.

On this unusual night with her father, she saw the silhouettes of the dancers moving together and apart above her head. She watched until her eyes started to burn. Only then did she become aware of heavy smoke that filled the air. The vapor bit into her lungs like a rodent. At the same time the music became unbearably loud and vulgar. It was late. The faces of the dancers had lost their former luster. They looked either ashen or had become purple from incessant movements and wine. The hair of the revelers was tousled and strands of its natural, blond or brown color appeared under their white, dusted wigs. Perspiration streaked satin skins. Some ladies' garments had become partly undone. They invited the eye to plunge into almost bare bosoms where the roses had faded. Gently, her father pulled her away. While she risked a last glance across her shoulder, she thought that if the floor would break from the constant trampling of so many feet, everyone would drown in wine.

* * *

All this happened many years ago. But would she ever know who her father was? She wondered as they continued to drive toward Yellowstone Park in the northwest of Wyoming. The young woman was now quite sleepy from lack of food and the long confinement in the car where her children chirped and pecked like birds. They were restless, cranky and hungry and made their needs known in whiny voices. Her daughter leaned against the Princeton man's shoulder and feeling safe there, tried to pull her brother's hair. The young woman had to move him out of harm's way and reprimand her daughter.

"He started it," the child replied angrily. The small girl's eyes grew even darker and more luminous as she challenged her mother. They still had not reached the sulphur springs of the park. Her beau had finished his beer and looked dreamily out the window where the foothills of Wyoming's mountains rapidly moved past them.

Without realizing it, she must have taken a brief nap. Her father was still driving. When she looked again at her lover's face, it now hung, as if separated from his body, in front of her.

Then with surprise and horror she noticed that the Princeton man's features were no longer just made of flesh and bone. Within his skin, inside his eyes, she saw an older man. He wore some type of uniform and his arms reached out for her. Yet before they could hold her, he slithered off a hill and onto a battlefield where he disappeared in a cloud of gun powder. The man within her lover had just kissed his wife farewell and had patted his small son on the head. It was a soldier off to a war and off to play the hero's role. He was once more going to portray a part that had become obsolete with Hector. The vision lasted only a moment but it tore the young woman's insides open. Once again she felt as if her face were being pushed toward the ground. As before, someone held her up by her legs while her head hung across the edge of a gaping hole. She was forced to look at a void that stretched bottomless below her. And she started to retch.

In the back mirror of the car her father caught her face that looked deathly pale. He quickly asked her:

"*Bist du krank?*" For a second she caught and held his eye, then she smiled vaguely. Her lips felt as if made of rubber. Silently, she shook her head. She could not speak. Dust choked her throat. The English sounds she wanted to form in order to reassure her Princeton man who did not perceive what was happening, did not come forth. After a while she seemed to hear music. They were just a few beats of a melody that repeated themselves over and over again until she finally distinguished the words, *L'ora ha sonata* . . .

She knew then that she would not get to the sulphur springs of Yellowstone Park. Nor would she ever see Old Faithful, the giant geyser that opened its eye once an hour and counted its sheep—much the way Polyphemus had observed his livestock before Odysseus blinded him. One-eyed Old Faithful looked wildly into the sun. It was the same cruel male sun that had stood threateningly above her in East Africa. There was no shade under which to hide. That day she knew she would not marry her Princeton man. She knew then she would not marry again, ever. Marriage, she thought in despair, was not for her.

VI

Mai Bela
(Give me water)

The bachelor and his sister had grown up at the edge of
New York without knowing their father except when he
visited them once a year, usually for a birthday. They were
only familiar with their mother's mental landscapes. For the
boy, some of those were so odd, so far removed from his
own masculine soul that he could not, or at most only to a
limited extent, identify with his mother's concepts and goals.
It took him a long time to understand how much he was like
her. What he had been able to see were mostly distorted
pictures. It was as if, while glancing at his face reflected
upon a lake, a wind rippled the surface of the water and
broke his radiant image so an eye rose here, a nose over there
and his forehead, white and generously curved, was below his
chin. The disconnected pieces frightened him. He preferred
not to look at himself at all. His mother found him sometimes
sitting in the middle of a room with his eyes closed. He
seemed to rely on his sense of touch and smell, the oldest
senses of all.

He loved water. Many mountains of Ethiopia are
volcanoes. Some of them contain hot springs that were
gathered in small and large pools. Over the years the young
woman and her children got to know most of them. Her
husband did not care for water. Not a good swimmer, he was
afraid of it. But he would sometimes drive his small family to
one of the springs that had developed into a spa and leave

98

them there for a week before he picked them up again.

The little boy, long before he knew how to swim, hopped at the slightest encouragement from his mother into the deep end of a pool. Popping up like a cork, his mother caught him laughingly before he sank again. He enjoyed the frogs and toads that often shared a large, tiled basin with him. Once in a while when for a moment nobody watched him, he caught a frog by its legs. When he was told to let his new, violently struggling toy go, he broke into angry tears and only reluctantly obeyed.

On sunny afternoons, his mother took him and his three-months-old sister whom she still breast fed to the Ghion Hotel of Addis Ababa. Its lovely gardens contained an Olympic-sized swimming pool sustained continuously by a hot, sulphur spring. From its thirty-foot high diving tower, free from flies and fleas that relentlessly pursued every warm blooded creature on the ground, one enjoyed a good look at acres of carefully enclosed land.

The large, walled-in landscape they admired from above contained the palace gardens of the Emperor. Here during all hours of the day several dozens of raggedly dressed gardeners and their helpers, some still children, looked after thousands of cultivated plants and flowers. Everywhere huge, green patches of lawns met the eye. Along their borders flaming red bougainvillea and purple orchids intermingled with yellow roses and tulips. Small woods of featherly acacias, tall Juniper trees, stunted oak, bundles of bamboo and old Sycamore trees could be seen everywhere in luscious abundance.

Sometimes, one of the Emperor's male lions that was kept as a symbol of his power, took a walk in the garden. Dignified and silent as if he had forgotten how to roar, the well nourished, blond-maned animal moved lazily on a long chain next to his guardian. He often was a thin soldier of the Imperial Bodyguard whose dirty, bare feet looked frail next to the lion's huge, softly padded paws. Aware of his supremacy, he kept his deadly claws well concealed.

On some weekends the bachelor's small family left the capital early on a Saturday morning and drove to Wollisso or Ambo where some of the hot springs were caught in prettily built pools. Especially the basin of Ambo was almost entirely composed of large, rough, volcanic stones. Its natural look greatly enhanced its attraction. The steamy water whose sulfuric content made it taste slightly salty, bubbled forth among black, glistening rocks and sturdy-stemmed Schola trees. Some of their strong, fleshy-leafed branches overhung the water. Those trees were the finest, natural diving boards one could wish for. It was much more fun to climb among their smooth, thick, gray-barked branches than any ladder leading toward a diving tower.

Some of the sulphur springs were sixty or seventy feet deep and poured not only into big pools but also filled thousands of bottles to be used as drinking water. It took a long time to replenish a sizable pool. Usually by the time the water reached the surface of the basin, it was no longer hot. During the cool mountain nights it got quickly cold. The chilly water discouraged a swim in some of the big, open-air pools during the rainy season. But the water of the smaller basins, those of Ambo and Wollisso, remained pleasantly warm. City people were welcome if they were willing to drive about two hundred miles south or west of Addis Ababa on sometimes hazardous roads flooded from pouring rain.

It was fashionable for some of the wealthy Greek, Armenian and Italian businessmen, as well as for British and American civil servants to spend weekends at Wollisso or Ambo, the spas that evolved around the hot springs. On special occasions there were also Russian military advisors and diplomats among the guests. The French and Germans were not missing either. During one of their visits the young woman and her husband met Gamal R., an Egyptian, married to a blond, athletic American. His considerably younger wife had all the hair Gamal's high forehead was missing. He had a Ph.D. in Political Science and worked for the Economic Commission of Africa whose main seat was built across the Emperor's palace in Addis Ababa. In his spare time the gifted Arab painted. With considerable talent. During their conversations it became quickly apparent that he had the refinement and articulation the young woman's husband did not.

The hotels usually made concessions toward gambling which was not allowed officially. During long, cool and often even chilly nights saturated with endless rain, sometimes large amounts of money were interchanged. The game rooms were heavily saturated with smoke and whiskey was not spared. The only furniture the rooms contained were green padded, square tables and chairs. Above each table hung a lamp whose narrow, bland shade threw its light only across the hands of the players. It left their faces and the rest of the room in darkness. The gamblers felt more comfortable in their protected privacy.

Once, after a weekend in Wollisso, the bachelor's father drove back to the city by himself. For several days he left his wife, children, nursemaid and Moushi, their female Pekinese, in Wollisso. They spent the week in almost total isolation since most guests returned to the capital and their various jobs as well. At dinner only a few hardened gamblers and one or two young wives with their children and servants, who remained standing behind the chairs of their small charges during the meal, could be seen in the largely empty dining room. The waiters, properly dressed but barefoot, stood most of the time next to a wall. Here they chatted in subdued voices with each other. Their eyes tried to anticipate any wish from their few guests before they were summoned to their tables.

As soon as the rain subsided a little, the young woman took her small children to the outdoor pool which they had to themselves most of the day. The few guests who were left at the hotel preferred to stay indoors to play bridge or backgammon. Some of the patrons even remained within their rooms while the sun was up and emerged only for dinner.

The hotel was a one-story brick building with a corrugated tin roof upon which the rain jumped in a mad dance. Constructed to last, it had been built by Italians around the turn of the century. Each room contained old, creaky furniture that was misshapen by the high humidity during the rainy season. The rooms were spacious and boasted dark, 14-foot ceilings that needed badly a new coat of paint. Their nicest feature was a sunken bathtub, almost a tiny pool in a room that contained a vast, curtained window. Small steps led down into the water that was held by massive granite blocks. Obsidians, the brittle, black glass stone of volcanic origin, intermingled with blank walls. If one looked closely, one could sometimes even see the faint purple of

101

amethyst. At all times the huge tub was filled to the brim with bubbling warm water from a thermal spring. On a rainy day, the children loved to paddle there after their nap in the afternoon and before they went to sleep at night.

But their mother wanted them also to get used to a larger body of water which they found only outdoors. On certain days when she felt especially active, she showed her children how one could lie on one's back on the surface of the water and be carried by it without having to move at all. Floating motionless on top of the water that was covered by white layers of vapor, her children thought she had turned part of the water into a plastic board on which she sunbathed. On a barely sunny day she got a red nose this way while the rest of her face and body remained white. The sun stood straight above their head and was extremely powerful even when it was mostly covered by clouds.

On a rare morning when it did not drizzle, the one-year-old little girl sat on top of the rough, unpolished stairs that led into the shallow end of the pool. Her tiny feet, pudgy and perfect, were impatiently curled inward. They were barely visible under the big bath towel wrapped around her shoulders. At this moment her toes, turned toward each other like fingers in a prayer, repeated the pattern of her father's feet. And even though the young woman knew her husband was quite far away, his silhouette seemed to rise from her daughter's feet until, like a jinn, he loomed larger than life behind the little girl.

The young woman shook her head as if she had been dreaming. Her daughter's feet showed how ready she was to imitate her brother and go back into the water at the faintest sign from her mother. The young woman had just swished her two-year-old son several times around herself before she let him plunge into the pool. She had held him by one arm and leg while she turned quickly around her own axis so the child's little tummy flew horizontally through the air before touching the water once more. Her son's giggles and happy screams spread a smile on his sister's face. She too wanted to participate in this game which could only be played in a couples.

Almas, the small Ethiopian nursemaid in her mid teens was standing at the edge of the pool next to the baby. When not holding a child, she laughed softly and clapped her hands while she watched the swimmers all morning. Almas, whose name means *black diamond* in Amharic, the official language of Ethiopia, did not go into the pool. With the exception of the Somali who dive laughingly into the shark-infested Red sea of Massava and Djibouti, most Ethiopians, born on lofty mountain tops, never learn to swim and are afraid of the water. The women use only the edge of a lake or a river in which to wash clothes or bathe. The rivers of Ethiopia are well stocked with crocodiles. Snakes and leeches are the least danger a swimmer is threatened with when he enters one of Ethiopia's beautiful lakes. Some of these large and serene bodies of water are saline and the home of thousands of pink flamingos. In contrast, pools were, apart from not living up to European or American health standards and containing various species of frogs, safe. But here Almas could not swim either.

According to her people's customs a one piece swimsuit, much less a bikini, is considered an indecent costume. The men who, as always, enjoy greater freedom than the women, are not criticized for putting on a short swim trunk. Yet it is inconceivable for most Ethiopian women, whether a Somali, a Shoa, a Danakil, a Kata Galla, a Tigre, or an Amhara to enter a public pool without wearing her ankle-length garment, called *kemis*. Her *kemis*, a dress with a full skirt, is usually white. Around her shoulders she often drapes a *natala*, a shawl with a matching *tibeb* border. Her simple white apparel and its intricate embroidery at its seams form a stunning contrast. *Kemis* and *natala* are rarely taken off. Even in the middle of the wildest, the most inaccessible country where the women bathe naked near the shore of a river or lake, they make sure they are in a secluded spot before they undress. It would take an Actaeon to catch a forbidden glimpse of a slender, brown Diana.

To wear clothes was not allowed in Wollisso's pool because the hotel management prided itself in adhering to European and American yardsticks. So Almas had to remain out of the water. Not able to swim, she was quite happy to walk up and down the length and width of the pool, to lift the struggling children out of the water, or let them slide in again. With her small nose and large, black eyes, the

103

extraordinary trademark of Ethiopian beauty, Almas had a pretty face. Her cheeks were full and in harmony with her round figure. Her body was close to the earth and solid. Her bare feet, nicely shaped and ending in long, immaculate toes, were at ease with the ground upon which they stepped. She was pleasant to watch even though she did not possess the haughty thinness of the Amhara. The young woman had never seen Almas without her hair tucked under a thin, black snood made of cotton. The headdress emphasized some of the Ethiopian's classical facial proportions whose Greek symmetry causes the heart to flutter. Almas had a friendly disposition and loved children. It was a love fully returned by her small charges. They easily picked up Amharic, Almas' ardous language whose alphabet consists of over two hundred thirty letters. Most foreign adults have a hard time to imitate its various guttural sounds that are unfamiliar to any European tongues.

The next morning in spite of a light rain mother and children frolicked once more in the warm water of the pool. Its steam mixed steadily with the humid air so one was not quite sure where one element ended and the other began. After a little while they were joined by a tall and slim Ethiopian in his early thirties. As he quickly walked past them at the edge of the pool, his attractive face made him look like a Somali or Tigrai from the north of Ethiopia. An excellent swimmer, the young man streamlined tirelessly from one end of the pool to the next. He swam silently and with concentration for almost an hour his innumerable laps and did not take any notice of his surroundings.

After his swim, he went back to the hotel, only to return a short while later, fully dressed. In spite of the constant fine rain, he sat down under a row of large euphorbias whose hundred arms spread toward the sky. A few garden chairs had been put under the thick, green foliage of the trees. Inadequately protected from the thin rain but not seeming to mind, he watched the woman and her children in front of him. His finely formed features did not try to hide his pleasure as he observed the scene. But he never said a word. After about half an hour, he bowed his head gracefully toward the young woman and left. In the evening he was not among the few other dinner guests. Yet the next morning he

104

swam in the pool again. Once more he surveyed in total silence the young mother and her children. That night again he was not among the other people of the hotel.

Only on the third day of their encounter did the stranger speak. As the young woman quickly discovered, Adamu Abebe was an officer of the Imperial Bodyguard. His wife and two children lived in Addis Ababa from which he had been exiled. The thirty-year-old captain shared his fate with many other soldiers of all ranks who had been involved in the coup d'état against Haile Selassi I late in 1960. Adamu was among the fortunate ones. He was not shot, nor hanged in public as some of the generals were. And he had survived his imprisonment where he had been submitted to frequent, brutal interrogations which had accumulated into many beatings. Some of these had been severe. Certain scenes were so ugly, he had buried them deep within himself. He was unable to live with them on a daily basis.

* * *

In December 1960 Haile Selassie I went on one of his many good will visits to Europe and the United States. Taking advantage of his father's absence, Asfa Wossen, his oldest son, tried with the help of the Imperial Bodyguard to overthrow the country. He was forty-five years old and had the round waistline of a middle-aged man. But he lacked his father's drawing power. With half of his life over, the short, stout prince still stood in the shadow of his dominant parent. Then one morning the crown prince had become tired of waiting for his father to abdicate.

For over forty years Haile Selassie I had ruled single-handedly his large nation. Literally on wings he had brought Ethiopia from the Middle Ages into the twentieth century by building airports, rather than roads, in his mountainous empire. DC-3's, the twenty-eight passenger planes, intersected Ethiopia from sunrise to sunset. Never at night. There were no facilities for it. This safe, two-engine plane was well adapted for taking off on fields slippery with rain. Most landing strips existed of grass and soil only. They often ended abruptly in a steep canyon. During the heaviest rains it was too perilous to land. A red flag signaled the danger and the plane only circled low over a small, shabby looking cabin that comprised the airport. Pilots needed special skills and a sixth sense devoted to the value of life. Yet even then some of the young, well trained flyers crashed. When help eventually arrived, not much of the plane or officer was left.

When passengers disembarked at the make-believe airports in the interior of Ethiopia, they continued their journey on mules, donkeys and small, sure-footed horses. The animals wore blinders so the crevasses remained hidden from them. With the assistance of the Swedes and the Americans, Haile Selassie I had founded an Air Force and a commercial airline of considerable success. It had not been an easy task to build airports among mountains ranging between 10,000 and 15,000 feet with Ras Dashan in the northwest peaking at 15,158 feet. Special planes were required. They had to be sturdy enough to take off and land in this altitude that competes with some of the highest, livable parts on earth.

Haile Selassie, who claimed to be the 220th descendant of King Solomon and the Queen of Sheba, reigned in Ethiopia with a bicameral parliament. But he ignored the parliament, and slyly, if need be brutally, he held on to power in a most unilateral way. For many complex reasons, some of which had to do with time and survival, he had become master in the game of ruling. He could no longer live without it, nor without the control and prestige that accompanied it, not to mention wealth. He was small and looked frail among his over six-foot, virile bodyguards who went with him everywhere. After a few years the little *Lion of Juda*, as he was called affectionately by his supporters, became inseparable from his throne. It was easier to imagine a turtle without its house than the Emperor without his country.

Cleverly he had reinforced his strength and shrewdness by marrying a woman of greater power than his own. Yet he remained loyal to his family who belonged to the elitists of Ethiopia, the Shoan-Amhara. Together with the handsome Tigrai, the Amhara who come from the region of Lake Tana and the Blue Nile, are Semites. They were centered in the Shoa province with Addis Ababa as its capital. The Amhara were in control of the military and most of the church which was, next to the Emperor, the second largest landowner of Ethiopia. Haile Selassie's father was *Ras*, meaning prince,

106

Makonnen of Harar, one of the great feudal lords. Patiently and ruthlessly the minute Emperor tried to legitimize his system within the political structure of a backward country that struggled to modernize itself.

In addition to being one of the wealthiest landowners of the world, Haile Selassie I had also accumulated large private funds. During his reign, rumors stubbornly persisted that he had several billion dollars safely stacked away in Swiss bank accounts. Meanwhile, Ethiopia's many peasants staggered on emaciated legs from drought into famine. Infant mortality was among the highest on earth.

There was no such thing as freedom of press or speech while Haile Selassie I ruled. In spite of the capital boasting several elementary schools, secondary schools, and even a university, illiteracy was still at 80%. The ones who could read took most texts literally, whether it was was the bible, a newspaper or a cook book. A certain amount of censorship was apparently necessary.

The Emperor felt protective about exposing his country's poverty. Mercilessly he had cameras confiscated as well as photos taken of public places that did not correspond to Western standards of industry and commerce. If one wanted, for instance, to photograph the *mercato* of Addis Ababa, which is the largest and most exotic market of East Africa, one risked being severely beaten by local policemen and having one's camera smashed.

The *mercato* was dominated by women. The sensual colors of their merchandise frequently displayed directly on the dry ground, were enticing. There were spices from the richest brown to the darkest red. The green of different sizes of beans spread everywhere. In the middle of vegetables and ripe fruits large and small baskets were piled up high. They were woven from grass and so well made that they often outlived the artisan whose clever fingers had labored over it. Invisible thoughts, dreams and desires had dwelled among the weavers' hands. Now they had become as concrete as the geometric designs in pale blue, fiery red and somber black of the woven container.

Holding a basket close to her nose the young woman imagined that she could smell those dreams. It was a unique scent one did not encounter anywhere else in the world.

When she looked up, she became once more involved in the picturesque market sights that were reinforced by a hundred odors. They clung sweetly and pungently to the air. The noise from donkeys, mules, sheep and bleating goats was deafening. And all over one saw bundles of live chicken that their owners carried by their feet while the poor, small heads of the birds dangled cruelly near the earth. Their cackles were hoarse from fear. In an obscure corner, among a heap of rubbish one could find a rare, hand-written bible with fastidious illustrations and illuminations. The small, leather-bound, immensely valuable book was bargained away for a few Ethiopian dollars. At a certain area a row of sewing machines were operated by men only. Their bare, bony feet pushed relentlessly a pedal. Working under a few protective wooden boards that opened toward the street and were attached to a shed, they looked dignified in their white jodhpurs and tunic. With their heads bent over their machines the handling of which was obviously a male privilege, the men pretended not to notice the watching crowd who surrounded them. If someone dared to ask a question, he was regally ignored for a long time. Laboring in public at the sewing machines was too important to allow any random interruption.

When the young woman was taken for the first time to the *mercato*, she thought she had stepped into a forgotten century. And even though in time the market, or at least certain sections of it, became familiar, it never lost its exotic thrill for her. Except when she went there with her mother-in-law. The Armenian's aggressive bargaining when she haggled over half a sheep or a lamb embarrassed the young woman. She felt sorry for the poor Ethiopian seller who was quickly outwitted by the clever Armenian. The old lady in turn did not take kindly to her daughter-in-law pitying the thin Ethiopian, dressed in rags. In her eyes that was a breach of loyalty to the clan. Ethiopians were an inferior race in the eyes of her mother-in-law. "You treat them fairly as domestics but you do not socialize with them," the Armenian told the young woman. "Do not waste any noble thoughts on these people. They do not appreciate them." She continued her narrow-minded lecture as the two women walked back to their car.

* * *

108

It must have been toward 2:00 pm one sunny afternoon. Later the bachelor's mother remembered the date and year: December 13, 1960. It was summertime in Ethiopia. For the moment, it looked like just another typical Ethiopian afternoon whose calendar counts thirteen months. The Ethiopian year has the same number of days as the European, but twelve months have thirty days and the thirteenth has five. For five months out of thirteen, rain pours on the flat tin roofs of Addis Ababa. It is a merciless, seemingly incessant rain that turns trucks into swimming barges and plays havoc with the soul, human and animal alike. Visions of the flood swirl in front of one's eyes. Rabies, still a frequent occurrence among dogs, hyenas and monkeys in cities and country alike, appears to strike more often during the rainy season.

During a wet August day one of the young woman's German shepherds whose finely tuned ears were more reliable than those of Tafari, their *zabania*, was struck by it. Usually loyal, intelligent and friendly, the dog suddenly bit the young woman and her sister who had come from New York for a prolonged visit. The mad canine then also attacked both of her children and Almas, the nursemaid. It happened quickly while they stood in a group in the courtyard next to several green banana trees. The women and children remained stunned while the dog fled in wild leaps toward the closed gate which he took in one desperate, giant jump. For several nights thereafter, the young woman heard the dog howling in the vicinity of her house. In the rain-soaked darkness she cried. Her arms hurt from the painful rabies shots. During five consecutive days she tried to calm down her screaming children in the doctor's office. Yet neither she nor her sister or Almas succeeded in consoling them while the physician's injections pierced skin and blood vessels. No shots hurt more than those to prevent rabies.

* * *

On a warm day in December 1960, the young woman had just teased their rhesus monkey with a banana, its favorite treat. She kept the bandar macaque, a smelly creature with its

109

narrow nasal septum, as a pet. It is as common in Ethiopia as the Hamadryas baboon and the Goreiza, the graceful, black and white colobus monkey that is mercilessly hunted for its fur. The macaque was chained to a Juniper tree in the garden. A thin wire spanned the distance from a branch to one wall of the house about twelve feet above the ground. Carrying a light metal chain attached to its leather collar, the little monkey constantly jumped off its tree and traveled on the ground as far as the wire permitted. Often like someone gone insane, it dashed back and forth on its wire and somersaulted on the lawn while it screeched on top of its lungs. One never knew whether it was mad or happy. The young woman was a little afraid of it, particularly of its thirty-two sharp teeth that penetrated the skin quickly, drawing blood. But she was fond of hearing her children's giggles and seeing their tiny stomachs shake with laughter when they watched the monkey perform its acrobatics among her carefully planted petunias, stocks, and mimosa.

The macaque shared the garden with an old, large turtle. Half the height of a Doberman pinscher, it had the face of a dragon and the soul of a lamb. Sometimes both children rode on its hard, broad back with space to spare. One day when the turtle was in search for food or freedom, the young woman found it sitting in her bedroom. It had climbed six long, narrow stone steps, then crossed a small veranda and an open door to get there.

A gazelle of Lilliputian size, perfectly proportioned and called *dig-dig*, sprang deftly around turtle and monkey. Its black hooves on which it walked as daintily as if wearing high-heeled dance slippers, were about as big as the thumbnails of three men.

The air was still that sunny afternoon. It was the hour of Pan. The world looked peaceful as it always did when the young woman's children took their afternoon nap. After she had gone back inside the house her eyelids started to feel heavy as she sat down and began to read.

Suddenly rifle shots came in short sequences. First they were quite far away as if a child were trying out a new toy. Curious the young woman stepped outside the front door to see what the noise was about. As she walked up and down the garden she still heard faint shots. Yet she was unable to discover anything. Then her English neighbor across the street called out to her,

"Close your shutters, get back indoors." The small English family was the only European one in the vicinity. The husband worked for the English Foreign Office and the young woman had become friendly with their pretty, pony-tailed, eight-year-old daughter who came over frequently to visit her. The little girl was fond of her children and liked to play mother to them. Once when the young woman and her small visitor were in the kitchen getting lunch ready, her infant daughter woke up in her room and started to whimper.

"Who is that cat crying?" the little English girl, pushing impatiently her blond hair out of her face, had wanted to know.

* * *

Shaking her head and stepping inside her house again the young woman beckoned to Yeshimabet, her *aschkarotsch*, her cook. She also called Tafari, their gardener and night watchman. The two lived with their families in a spacious hut in the back of the compound. Tafari had a wife, named Mulu. She was a quiet, elfin thing who in spite of three small children, looked more like a girl than a woman. Mulu did not work in the house. Each time the young woman approached the open door of her cabin, she shyly receded into its background. The two women rarely spoke to each other.

Yeshimabet, or Yeshi for short, whose full name means *Mistress over a thousand People*, was full bosomed, intelligent, and articulate in Amharic. She also could make herself understood in Italian. Without the help of a husband she raised two daughters on her own. One of them was still an infant. Well fed, the baby always wore a knitted, woolen hat that had once belonged to the young woman's own daughter.

During the quiet hours of the day and at night or whenever they were not needed in the house, the servants went to their own living quarters from where soon the delicious odor of *wott*, cooked over an open fire, rose and tickled everyone's nose.

The unprotected fire was built on the floor and

dangerous. A year ago the four-year-old daughter of Tafari and Mulu had fallen into it and burned herself badly. The young woman who heard the child's terrible screams had wanted to rush it to the hospital. But Tafari said:

"It's only a girl. If God wants it, let her die."

Mulu did not open her mouth but her eyes that seemed huge in her gray-black face were fastened on the young woman's face. It was clear she did not expect any mercy from the father of her endangered child. Help had to come from the white woman.

It was not cruelty that had made Tafari speak this way but tradition and fear of high hospital costs he would have only risked for one of his sons. Not for his daughter. Daughters were cheap. Until they reached their teens and could be married off to a suitor who had to pay his future father-in-law for his bride, girls were considered useless even though they helped their mothers to do most of the work in the house.

At Tafari's words anger quickly rose in the young woman and her first impulse was to strike him. Instead, she dug her long fingernails into the palm of her hands and patiently explained to him that all expenses would be taken care of by her and her husband. Finally, after the horrible wailing of his child became unbearable and the young woman thought she could no longer keep her temper, Tafari reluctantly agreed to have his daughter taken to the hospital. They quickly got into her car. Even though she used her horn almost constantly and drove as fast as she dared, the heartrending whimpers and suffocated shrieks of the child were insupportable. Tafari never said a word.

It took months for the skin of the little girl to heal. Almost the entire right side of the child, arm, hip and thigh, as far as the knee, were burned. The first two skin grafts did not take and the small girl in spite of morphine shots was for hours in agony. Then after she finally came back home, she did not play with the other children right away. Like an injured bird who had fallen out of its nest, she sat apart from her brothers and watched them apprehensively from under her long lashes.

* * *

112

On December 13, 1960 after the first shots had fallen the young woman together with her servants quickly fastened the wooden window shutters of the house. She also made sure that the main gate, hanging loosely on its hinges and needing repair, was closed as tightly as possible. Hardly back in the house, the shots came closer. The young woman and her household seemed to smell the exhaust pipes of jeeps and trucks. After a short while, they all heard the shuffling of many running feet. Wide-eyed, Yeshi and Almas asked the young woman again and again what this strange commotion, which had begun to frighten them, was all about. Tafari just watched her. But his dark eyes in a narrow, symmetrical face followed her movements closely. Yet he did not speak to her. He waited for her husband whom he alone acknowledged as the master. In any event, it was clear to him that the young woman did not know what was going on.

Their home, the last one in a twisting, partly hidden dead end street, was enclosed by a small grove of Eucalyptus trees. Buried like a mossy stone in a small stream the house lay at its bottom. Their concealment was their only protection. Inside the house telephone and electricity had been cut off almost at the same time. The young woman tried to call her husband and then her neighbor across the street. Their house sat on a low hill and was more exposed. The line was dead. The radio did not function either. She did not know what to do.

By this time the rifle shots were very close to the house. But the young woman's children were still asleep. Yeshimabet had brought her five-year-old daughter and the six-month-old baby whom she carried on her hip through the back door into the kitchen. Her mistress noticed that patches of gray started to appear among the dark brown skin of Yeshi's face. She looked half beseechingly, half angrily at the young woman and hugged both of her children close to her. The older girl who already helped her mother was crying. Shamefacedly, she hid her head in her mother's skirt when the young woman tried to pat her thin shoulders.

Even Tafari, who almost never entered the house, put his wife and three children there. Most of them sat silently on the floor of the kitchen. They started to huddle together and now, as the shots were outside the front gate, fear began to weave in almost visible threats in and out of their group. No one knew what was happening. They were only intensely aware of shots and shouts of rage, of savage joy and of pain coming close, until the uproar seemed to swing like the screeching monkey outside from tree-top to tree-top. Each shot heightened their terror of the unknown now all around them. Distress reduced their voices to whispers. They felt like ants upon whose hill a human foot was about to descend.

When the shots came through the fence and some of them were hitting the thin walls of their house, walls made of twigs and dried earth, the young woman did something totally unaccustomed. It was as if she obeyed a voice softly rising and inaudible to others, from a forgotten past. She got up and left the kitchen after she had taken a stool from it. Slowly she placed it in the middle of their square entrance hall. Then she got hold of one of her husband's guns and sat down, facing the main door. Without moving she stared at the thick, opaque glass inset that was part of the door.

No longer saying a word because she was afraid if she opened her mouth she would scream, she quietly waited for what seemed an interminable length of time. Straight and motionless she sat. Only her fingers kept imperceptibly caressing the cold, smooth steel in her lap. She remained with her back turned toward her children's room. In spite of Yeshi's and Almas repeated pleas, she had forbidden them to wake either her son or daughter.

She did not know how to shoot, but she was certain she could pull the trigger at the first man coming through the front door. She knew she would have only one chance. Robberies were almost always committed by bands of at least ten to fifteen men. They usually occurred at night, but one could never tell. Judging from the terrifying noise outside their compound, there must have been an entire army of *shiftas*, the dreaded bandits. They seemed to loot house after house.

She nearly killed her husband. Somehow he had managed to get from his office that was located midtown, to their home at the outskirts of Addis Ababa. He had driven crazily. His foot was almost silmultaneously on the gas pedal and brake. He hopscotched like a wildly excited child and bowed

114

behind his steering wheel to avoid flying bullets that came from left and right. Finally, he made it through the midst of the civil war. Nothing less than that was going on. The fight lasted for three horrible days.

* * *

The Imperial Bodyguard under the disguised leadership of the crown prince and Ras Imru, a close cousin of Haile Selassie I fought the Imperial Army. At first not sure which way to turn, the army decided to remain loyal to the Emperor. Mengistu Neway, the commander of the six-thousand men Imperial Bodyguard led the insurrection. He was helped by his younger and more radical brother Gerame, governor of Wellamo, a division of the Sidamo province. Both brothers belonged to the Moja family of the Shoa province. Their distinction and wealth were based, as those of most Ethiopian nobles, upon large possessions of land. For generations the Mojas had been connected with the imperial line. They had held important administrative posts throughout the empire. Their political and social influence was to be reckoned with. But in the recent past their loyalty to Haile Selassie I had been questioned several times.

That evening and several hours during the next three days, most of the household members spent lying under the dining room table. With its glass and china-packed hutches lined up against the walls, this room was the only semi protected place in a house that had no basement or cellar. Their beds were too close to the windows and threadlike walls to guard them from harm, even if they had crawled under them.

VII

Adamu Abebe
(Portrait of an officer)

On December 16th, 1960, three days after the coup, the Emperor's plane with its golden-green *Lion of Juda* painted in gigantic proportions on the fuselage of a DC-6B landed in Addis Ababa. In spite of the fact that the airport was closed. The little king of kings, his aristocratic face hidden under the mask of his black beard and bushy eyebrows, rode through his capital's streets as if his people had prepared the usual triumphant welcome. It was a salute he was now accustomed to. After forty-four years of ruling his country as a medieval autocrat, or at least as an enlightened despot, he knew his people. Even after they had lost their heads. It took courage to walk into a wasps' nest. For even though the Imperial Army under the leadership of General Merid Mengesha and Major General Kebede Gebre had the abortive coup fairly well under control, the crisis was not over.

The adept handling of an incident like this and other minor political upheavals had established Haile Selassie's I reputation as the most powerful and clever politician among the African nations. Part of this invincibility he had achieved by putting himself at the apex of an Imperial palace structure. The carefully construed arrangement had only one purpose—to worship the patriarch. Starting with Asfa Wossen, the crown prince, everyone bowed deeply in front of this image.

The Emperor could have remained in safety outside of

116

Ethiopia. He could have waited until the storm had blown over and not take the risk of his being swept away by it. Instead he became the storm itself. Like a black cloud, his well-known Rolls Royce without a license plate, slowly floated through the main streets of Addis Ababa. It was a long way from the airport to the palace. He moved slowly. Wherever he passed the people bowed low, like grass in the wind. Their heads touched the ground. Their bodies sunk to their knees and fell flat on their stomachs until they had paid full tribute to their ideal.

Thousands of peasants, their lot worse than those of Russian serfs before 1917, dropped on their knees and on the dust of the road. As their flea and lice infested, thin bodies dressed in rags lay in the dirt of the street, their simple souls were set aglow by the Emperor. They identified with the man, the human being whose clean-scrubbed and perfumed flesh was vulnerable and whose blood was like theirs. Even more, they identified with the Emperor's shadow, his dark splendor that was, they firmly believed, three thousand years long.

During that deep stretch of time the representations of the Queen of Sheba and King Solomon had lasted. Reinforced by numerous wooden paintings that hung above worn straw mats in Coptic churches the images of queen and king had floated on their legendary stems through the minds of the people. The exterior of the Emperor, his small, feeble figure dressed in a highly decorated uniform was a gilded mirror that reflected their dreams. By prostrating themselves in front of him, their noses only inches away from cow manure and donkey dung, the people whose stomachs growled audibly, became part of him.

He was the golden vision that lived in the tenebrous depths of their souls. He, a frog like them had climbed up slowly the ladder of evolution. He had maimed and murdered his rivals and had become a prince. On some special occasions, like this one now, even the poorest man, starving and eaten alive by amoebas and leprosy, dared to walk through this golden mirror held up in front of him and a thousand others. With their bare, dirty feet, they broke the glass and faced the Cimmerian shade beyond it. Within the center of blackness they saw the symbol of the Emperor, the

117

glittering idol that floated god-like above them. They were terrified. Their abhorrence was like the one in front of a snake ready to strike them a deadly blow at any moment. Yet next to the serpent, they also saw a white dove that softened their dread. They never knew what they should revere more, power and murder, or wisdom and gentleness, wrapped up in one image.

For millions of Ethiopians Haile Selassie I was a godly figure, a reincarnation of century old Church paintings. Vast-eyed, he had walked out of his wooden frame. To his country he was a vestige from Roman times when the symbol of emperors loomed in stone and highly polished marble behind living flesh and when the eyes of most citizens did not dare to rise above a knee for fear their god's mouth would pronounce death over them. In his poor people's eyes the petite Emperor whose feet, unless supported by a stool and thick pillows, dangled helplessly in the air as he sat on his velvet throne, was also the Blakian patriarch with a flowing beard. He was in command of visible and invisible satanic powers. For his people he became the prehistoric, barbaric, powerful hero who had unfastened himself from the cross. Somehow he had pulled the nails out of his hands and feet and walked the terrible ground once more. He was the living god whose gentle sweep of hand caused death or bliss.

Asfa Wossen, the crown prince, never had a chance as he waited behind the curtains for his father to step out of the spotlight. Soft, potbellied, less ferocious and intelligent than his father and quite lazy, he did not like to climb ladders. Compared with his ascetic-looking father, he was like the frog princeling who lives concealed on the bottom of a forgotten well.

Even though it was known throughout the country that Asfa Wossen was at the heart of the *coup d'état*, his father could not execute him. It would have caused difficulties on various political, social and emotional levels. But several heads rolled. In great disgrace General Mengistu was hung publicly. His brother committed suicide. Four hundred seventy-five members of the Imperial Bodyguard were killed in the counterattack issued by the Imperial Army. Over three thousand soldiers and officers were arrested. For about two months, the *Ethiopian Herald* daily published new accounts of court trials, imprisonments, banishments and suicides. Four weeks after the violent seizure the main city streets were blocked by marching penitents—students, governmental and landed officials—anybody who was slightly implicated or connected with the overthrow was force-paraded to the palace. Its heavy, baroque gates were guarded by two mounted officers. Their ostentatious red and gold uniforms and the way they sat straight-backed and mute on their steeds reflected their English counterparts in front of Buckingham Palace. Added to the soldiers and horses outfits were taste and style of an oriental potentate. Without blinking an eye and with only their even-tempered animals switching a tail to ward off ever present flies, the guards stonily watched a sea of heads bend and sway and swear total allegiance to the Emperor. As their lips moved and their mouths twitched, no one could see into the depth of their hearts. There were many who hated the Emperor and craved change.

The Imperial Guard, carefully trained to defend the Emperor, lay in shreds. Haile Selassie I was reinstated and reclined a little deeper into the red silk cushions of his throne. As he leaned back with a sigh, his left leg tried not to lose touch with the heavy pad put under it. At least when sitting down, he attempted to look taller than he was.

Justice, or what was considered as such, was dispensed and shortly after many had died, the Emperor attended public and social affairs as if nothing had happened. Only those who saw him closely, detected that his lips were shut more firmly and that he lifted his right hand more haughtily. And the lines on his imposing forehead resembled more than ever thin, writhing snakes.

* * *

Adamu Abebe considered himself fortunate to be alive. Within a few days after the abortive coup he had been arrested, imprisoned and questioned. For about two weeks, as he was beaten again and again, he had feared for his life. Mutely, he lay on a rag in the corner of his cell. His body was badly cut and bruised. The skin on his shoulders and upper arms where whip and rod had descended most frequently was broken. In some places to the bone. Flies sat on the coagulating blood. He did not bother to chase them away. Every movement intensified his agony. And the flies, too many of them, returned within moments. Worse than the intense physical pain was the agony of his mind. At any hour of the day, often after midnight when he had just fallen into a restless sleep, the kick of a boot in his ribs woke him. Arms stronger than his dragged him through a long, squalid hall into another room for further interrogations and intimidations, for more cruel blows, more shouts and more screams. Helplessly, he was caught in a living nightmare. Every moment, awake or asleep, he had to dread for his life. There was no one to protect him.

* * *

The prisons of Ethiopia lack certain comforts the jails in Europe and the United States possess. Such commodities as beds, tables, chairs, shelves, toilets, radios, television and showers are not included. Only the wealthiest inmates own a mattress that a considerate relative brought for them. Not before he payed a hefty bribe to the guards. During the day this priceless possession serves as a table, a chair and a storage place. Neither do Ethiopian prisons have courtyards for daily exercises, a doctor's office nor a library. There is no kitchen either or any type of food for that matter. Poor inmates without family or friends to bring them something to eat and money to pay the prison warden, slowly starve to death.

Even Akaki, the most modern prison of the country located near the center of the capital and in the middle of an affluent neighborhood still holds on firmly to Medieval and Renaissance customs such as rags on the floor, mice, rats, lice and fleas. These pests multiply in great abundance under the favorable conditions of perpetual foulness. And they carry diseases with them. During the rainy season worms crawl on the mud floor. Hundreds of them. Thick, slimy and loathing to the point of eliciting bouts of vomit, they come through holes in the corrugated-metal walls and leaky roofs. They are so numerous that prisoners cannot avoid stepping on their squirming bodies. The prison boasts only one luxury—an

120

electric chair. It sits separately in a small, beige building. At a moment's notice it is ready for its next victim.

Daily around noon a group of men, women and children huddle on the ground outside the jail. They are relatives or friends of the convicts. Usually squatting under a large, black umbrella that serves equally well against a strong sun or pouring rain, they wait uncomplainingly.

At 12:00 noon one of the prison guards comes to the gates and barks a command. The person closest to the gate, mostly a woman or young girl, timidly steps forward and with several deep bows, hands a small parcel through the tall iron gate that has been opened a few inches. The guard, who does not look at the donor, takes the food, walks away, returns after a little while and, full of his own importance he struts along and calls out the next person in line. Since there is only one guard and many relatives, the ritual takes a long time, which is precisely what protocols are all about. By taking only one container of food at a time the guard fulfills at least two important functions.

First, he justifies his job. He is the highest paid sentinel since he is the only visible link between the captive and the outer world. Food is distributed just once a day. Without it the prisoner dies. Second, by taking one parcel at a time, the ward vividly demonstrates his honesty. He supposedly brings the food immediately to the detainee then returns empty-handed to take the next food ration. Everyone knows this guardian is less honest than he claims to be. So in addition to the bread and meat carefully wrapped in a cooking utensil, money is often slipped into his hand to make sure the prisoner gets at least part of the meal prepared by his family. The household of the inmate is often desperately poor and does not have much to eat either.

* * *

For at least two weeks Adamu Abebe was too ill and in too much pain to pay attention to food. The small pot put next to him and fastidiously enclosed in a thin, white cotton cloth was ignored by him. He knew it contained *doro wott*, a chicken stew served with boiled eggs. He loved this dish which is cooked with berbere, a hot, red pepper. This spice

121

constitutes a major source of vitamins for most Ethiopians. Even though the food smelled delicious Adamu's stomach started to retch when he thought of eating.

Only during his last three months of imprisonment when he was no longer tortured, did he look forward to noon and the most important event of the day. He knew his wife supervised the making of *injera*, the flat, soft Ethiopian bread made of *tef* and called *Eragiostic Abyssinia*. The grain is mixed with water and poured in a thin streak on a wide hot dish made of clay and dung. The bread takes only a few minutes to cook and is savory hot or cold. Thirsty, Adamu hoped the guard did not take all of the *tej*, a sweet wine made from an intoxicating mixture of honey, water and the leaves of *gesho* or *Rhamnus prinoides*. Carefully, Ethiopians carry it everywhere in a small, pot-bellied, hollow, yellow gourd. He would have loved to get hold of a handful of *quat*, *Celestrus edulis*, the light-green leaves that grow wild in the hills around Harar. The plant abolishes hunger and promises feverish dreams where colors and forms take on unknown seductive distortions. Lying motionless in his corner, he could almost see himself chewing the fresh leaves and could imagine their hallucinating effect. The *quat* and *tej* or *tala*, a beer made from barley, would have helped him to forget his sorid surroundings. He might have not been so conscious of the penetrating outcries in the night, the shouts of the guards, and the horrible sounds of a whip descending upon exposed, vulnerable flesh.

Sometimes in the past, just a few sips of *tej* had allowed him to flow upon the river of memory. Like a salmon, he then retraced his steps and swam strongly against the current until he reached places where he had lived as a child and young adult.

* * *

His youth had been a promising one. Son of a minor noble who lived near Axum and Adowa, his father had been able to send him to the Military Academy in Harar.

From the time when Islam started to expand until almost the 20th century Harar paid heed to its religion with fanatic passion. The walled city that nestles among mountains has

122

close to a hundred mosques and ranks fourth highest among the holy cities of Islam. Until not too long ago non-moslems, if they were discovered among the walls of Harar, were killed. Even the British explorer, Sir Richard Francis Burton, when he attempted in 1855 to visit the city in disguise, nearly lost his life.

Axum, in whose vicinity Adamu was born, is Ethiopia's most timeworn city. It was here where the Queen of Sheba had once reigned. Her bath can still be seen not too far from the graves of King Kaleb and King Gabre Meskel, making it one of the most visited sights. Bath and tombs are perhaps only rivaled by Axum's 16th-century Cathedral of St. Mary of Zion, built on the spot of a church that goes back to the forth century. The cathedral is not only a place where crowns, once owned by some of Ethiopia's former emperors, are stored but it also—so most Ethiopians believe—contains the original Ark of the Covenant. This legendary treasure makes it priceless in the eyes of the Coptic church that is predominant in Ethiopia.

Axum's extraordinary obelisks or stelae go back to the Sabaen and the Byzantine periods. Carved from single blocks of granite they incarnate multi-story buildings. The tallest, now laying in pieces, once exceeded ninety feet. The highest obelisk that still towers above the city's other buildings is close to seventy feet tall. Geometrical patterns are cut deeply into the stone. They show accurately the beams for each floor and the windows.

* * *

Adamu was proud of those colorful legends and historical facts. They reinforced his tradition-bound past. Adowa, only twenty miles from Axum, had taught him the most important lesson in politics and geography a modern Ethiopian knows, the defeat of the Italians in 1895. Adowa and Axum were part of Tigre, the towering, wild, almost inaccessible mountain range in the north of Ethiopia where it borders Eritrea.

Already as a child, he had learned about Menelik II, the predecessor of Haile Selassie, and his empress. Before the decisive battle against the Italians the heavy woman dressed in brocade did public penance by carrying an enormous stone on her back when she implored heavenly help for victory. The royal couple was supported by loyal soldiers. Though they were bare-footed and emaciated, the Ethiopian fighters with their spears, large knives and a few gun-carrying men, outran the far better-equipped Italian battalions. The advantage of the Ethiopians was their superior knowledge of the difficult terrain and their larger than normal lungs. Where the Italians lost their breath after a few steps, the Ethiopians were able to inhale the sparse mountain air with ease. The Italians had marched into Ethiopia from the Red Sea under appalling conditions. It took months before they met with the enemy. By then their army had lost a third of its soldiers to malnutrition, diseases and skirmishes with small bands of *shiftas* (robbers). Also the Italians had no maps and quickly got lost in the middle of a hostile mountain world where their numbers were dispersed and killed before they had been aware of what loomed around the next boulder they had to pass.

Adamu was also fond of Harar, the most flamboyant city of Ethiopia, still tightly embraced by its medieval walls and together with Gondar, one of the former capitals. In his mind rose the ruins of the Castle Anbesa, the Lion Palace, built by Ras Makonnen for Menelik II. Leaning against the damp, filthy prison wall, his hands could almost touch the carved lions sitting on the rampart where they kept watch with stony eyes.

He was well familiar with a two-story house, now a Moslem school, that was encircled by a large courtyard. Arthur Rimbaud, the child poet, who had written everything there was to write by the time he was twenty-one, had lived here. Visionary and disillusioned, Rimbaud chose a life of adventure and defamation. Far away from home, he ran guns and got involved in slave-trading, anything to make money. Star of the Symbolist movement and someone who put new meaning into poetry, he preferred the life of an opportunist and tried in vain to become rich. He almost did but a tumor in his knee forced him to return to France. Even though his leg was amputated there, he died in September 1891 in Marseille. He was thirty-seven years old. One of the streets in Harar still bears Rimaud's name. French used to be the

124

second language of this exotic city where an old, skinny Ethiopian feeds every night wild hyenas he coaxes to a dirty, brightly illuminated wall.

Lying asleep on the hard, foul smelling floor of his prison cell, Adamu dreamt about one of his former instructors, a tall, white-blond Swede. He had first pointed out to Adamu the ornate, old Arabic archway in Harar under which Sir Richard Francis Burton, the great traveler and friend of Queen Mentwab, had passed. Not far from it was the Faras Magala Square and the Mosque of Jamai, two reminders of the Ottoman Bank that had been located there during the nineteenth century.

Adamu had spent three years at the Military Academy, the Ethiopian equivalent of West Point. The simple buildings of the institution spread all over the outer town of Harar. A colonel from Bombay had headed the school, but his instructors included officers from Sweden, Canada, the United States and Britain. Haile Selassie I wanted to make certain that his officers of the Imperial Bodyguard and the Imperial Army were trained in the best possible way.

To be sent to the capital, the seat of the Emperor, was a promotion. It was an exterior sign of distinction like wearing a golden Phi Beta Kappa key. Most Ethiopian officers and aristocrats strove for that. Yet only a few, only the elite or people with connections, reached the "New Flower," the meaning of Addis Ababa in Amharic. In some ways Haile Selassie I was to his country, which is one of the largest on the African continent, what Louis XIV had been to France and Europe.

The Grand Palace of Addis Ababa was yet another imitation of Versailles. The architecture of the Emperor's royal residence hardly resembled Versailles, but it was as much a center of power as the sun king's sumptuous castle had once been. The Grand Palace had its gilded halls and on its spacious lawns young, male lions stalked among marble sculptures and immaculately swept drive ways. Even Louis XIV had not kept the long-maned beasts as pets. Haile Selassie I, in the midst of princes, princesses and educated, pretty concubines, was as wise, as worldly, as vain and as clever as his famous French predecessor. Cunningly, he surrounded himself with the best advisors, the finest artists, and the most distinguished nobles whose egos he fanned while he diminished their power.

Some concealed parts of the Little Lion even resembled Mallarmé's *l'araignée sacrée* who creates its own universe. The minute ruler was a creature so mysterious, so quixotic and he needed so little air as he explored forbidden worlds where most people feel as if invisible hands choke them that only a small group of initiates, a handful of chosen disciples, was able to comprehend and support him. There were people who saw the short Emperor as the embodiment of Tasso's, Herder's, Jean Paul's, Goethe's and most of all Nietzsche's *Übermensch*, man in the consciousness of his completeness, the ideal human, the way the Renaissance saw man and Ariosto depicted him in his *Orlando Furioso*.

The Emperor's advisors understood, or at least came one day to the perhaps somewhat forceful conclusion that unusual powers require abnormal laws, certain atypical responsibilities, and bizarre forms of freedom. Not everyone is capable of walking on top of skyscrapers or at the outer edge of a roof that is unprotected by a fence. The slightest step in the wrong direction and one must be able to fly or perish. The one who lives on roof tops has to obey different laws of gravity. He must be capable of mocking himself and follow his own instincts that are stronger, nobler and more brutal than those of other men who—as the myth tells us—are born equal and who prosper under the law, or at least adhere to it.

* * *

To his great disappointment Adamu Abebe, instead of being called to Addis Ababa, was sent to a desolate village at the foot of Amba Geshen about three hundred miles north of the capital. As a full-fledged officer of the Imperial Bodyguard, he enjoyed the privileges due his rank and background. But there was no one to impress.

The peasants, including the headman or *shum*, who lived in the few *tukuls*, the conical mud and thatch huts that comprised the village, had always worked under an overlord. It mattered little to the villagers who it was. They toiled the earth, tended their goats and their rickety, vermin infested, velvet-eyed, long-horned cattle and paid their heavy dues. Most of the farmers' animals and the crops they raised belonged to their landlord. They did not own the land upon which they worked. They were grateful Adamu Abebe only occasionally staged a hunting party and that he had no ambition to build a road or erect a school, a church, or a government building. The peasants were the ones who paid for each new idea by which one of their squires was inspired. The poor villagers were not reimbursed in money. Only small plots of land were leased to them on which they could grow their own produce.

The peasants and their families were born to bear a man like Adamu Abebe. So accustomed had they become to their intolerable burden that they no longer questioned it. Lincoln was an unknown personage to these forsaken people who were unable to read. They only knew that men were born into a class system and remained there unless an earthquake, a famine or a revolution uprooted them. They considered themselves fortunate if they became forty years old. Most of them did not. Even in the capital, small cities and towns where there was more food and medication, a large proportion of Ethiopians died before they reached their 40th birthday. Those who were deprived of becoming forty years old and did not reach the level where other Homo Sapiens start to get some control over their own lives, did not get any compassion from their more fortunate fellow men. Instead, with a quick shrug of the shoulder, they were brushed aside as being too lazy, too squalid or too stupid to deserve any better.

Next to some perfectly preserved building like a church of medieval architecture, a magnificent emblem of humanity, hands and feet were ruthlessly stepped upon. Darwin's law, the survival of the fittest, was cruelly, daily and more visibly demonstrated here than elsewhere throughout most of the world.

* * *

Often at sunset Adamu Abebe listened to the plaintive cry of a flute that one of the young, delicate herdsmen played. Like a spirit from the past the lovely sound rose

127

against the sky. Imperceptibly, the melody vanished among the splendid crowns of acacia trees that stood in front of the blue walls of mountains. As he leaned back in his chair and sipped his Chianti or white Burgundy, not *tej* or *talla* that his peasants occasionally drank, he thought he saw a faint outline projected onto the quickly darkening horizon. As he looked on, the design formed an almost invisible silhouette that resembled the Emperor. While the sun slipped blood-red between the partition of mountains that hung like a stage curtain in front of him, his heart clenched. It was as if the two tiny fists of an infant who lived below his throat were holding his heart in the spasm of a temper tantrum. At those moments he became aware that his life dripped away drop by drop like a leaking bottle. Wherever his hands reached, in whatever place his fingers groped, they held only air and dust.

Days away from the next small town, there was nothing in Adamu's forgotten village except the specter of the Emperor. His fleshless contours hung like a star in the sky. Below his deity there was he, not yet twenty-five years old, a bachelor and sitting in the midst of nowhere. He was enclosed by tiny *tukuls* that took shelter at the foot of mountains whose restrictive curves were interrupted by phallic shaped, hostile *ambas*. A few of those high, slender rocks with their crests flattened out had formed natural basins here and there to gather rain water. It was urgently needed for the monks who chose to live on one of these inhabitable formations. Utterly forlorn, the *ambas* stood in an empty, grandiose landscape. Every evening before nightfall when the children's cries had subsided and only a dog barked once in a while, Adamu looked at the cold ground before him until he thought his eyes were turning into metal. In the dark no one saw the tears that streamlined the smooth skin of his face and moistened his exquisitely shaped, dark red lips no woman kissed.

If Adamu wanted some intelligent conversation, he had to climb seven hundred and three steps to visit the monks who had settled long ago on top of Geshen, one of the *ambas*. The monks lived the life of prisoners. Once they climbed the mountain, they never left it. Frugal and pious, they were still steeped in the 16th and even earlier centuries.

But in spite of their obsolete and secret world, the cenobites held onto, they could read and were capable of communicating with the young officer, a solace he had to forego with his tenants. Adamu enjoyed talking to the monks. He listened attentively to their softly and slowly spoken words that seemed full of peace his own restless soul was missing. Even more, he liked to watch the abbot and anchorites perform their various rituals.

One day he was invited to stay the night and was privileged to watch the monks at sunrise. At the horizon the first blush of dawn threw its light across the still starry sky. But the monks had already lined up in an orderly manner and started to take a walk. In the pure, chilly air that lacked oxygen, one black-cloaked monk after another marched in measured steps yet briskly behind each other on a well marked path. The long, dark line was headed toward the edge of the *amba*. There the cliffs dropped away under their feet for hundreds of yards. Looking down, Adamu's eyes started to swing crazily from left to right. His eyes flew across the empty space like a trapeze artist until they came to a halt on top of a sturdy bush that concealed the abyss below. When the monks could not go any farther, they stopped in front of a row of small outhouses. These were built directly over the gorge like the flying buttresses of a cathedral. With time to spare, calmly and unconcerned about the depth below him, one monk after another disappeared in the *bathhouse* and cleansed himself while leaning across nothingness as if he were a pigeon on the roof of Notre Dame. As they waited for each other, they began to sing. It was a simple chant that went straight to the heart.

Adamu did not visit the holy men on a regular level. The climb was steep and strenuous. Each step he took propelled him forward in his physical ascent. But inwardly, as his thoughts twirled about in the thin mountain air and while his breath came and went in abrupt, sharp puffs, he descended into Ethiopia's long past. Slowly, like a big salmon, he struggled against the current. He first stumbled across Johnson and Milton. The latter had integrated *Amba Geshen*, a typical, sharply pointed Abyssinian mountain, into *Paradise Lost*. Milton had encountered *Amba Geshen* in Purchase's travel literature. Samuel Purchase had been an English

129

clergyman and chaplain to the archbishop of Canterbury. When he no longer pursued his pilgrimages throughout the world, he became rector of St. Martin's Church. That was in the early 17th century.

Adamu retraced his steps even further. Panting in the crystal air, but having climbed only about three hundred steps, he met Alvarez, the Portuguese, who reported that *Amba Geshen* was a mountain where princes were kept prisoners. That was in 1520. Alvarez had captured Europe's imagination by his vivid description of Ethiopia.

The Portuguese sketched stories like those of an escaped prince who had been caught in Lalibela and got the tip of his nose cut off. This appalling punishment was used to prevent him from ever becoming king. No mutilated monarch could rule. After his cruel chastisement the weeping prince was taken back to his prison on top of *Amba Geshen*. Alvarez claims he briefly saw the prince. He was tightly guarded by thirty soldiers whose lives guaranteed the safe return of their noble charge. To conceal the identity of the prince, a black, coarse cloth was thrown over him and the mule he rode. To anyone who passed him and his escort on their long, harsh journey, only four eyes and two long, furry ears were visible.

In addition to being a prison, the mountain, also called *Amba Israel*, had served as a repository of the king's treasure. That was in the fourteenth century.

A hundred years before Alvarez, Fra Paez, a gifted Jesuit who built the Palace of Suseneyos at Gorgora and wrote a history of Ethiopia, reports that King Yekun Amlac imprisoned his five sons on Geshen in 1225.

Amba Geshen, together with the holy hills of Debra Tabor and Wahni, was one of the three mountain prisons where the offspring of kings were put when they reached adolescence. That way, sons of queens and concubines could not endanger the life of the king in power. The prison was a fresh water pool where, whenever the occasion arose, a successor of the bloodline, a young, faceless frog, could be quickly taken. Only one out of a hundred princes was chosen, the others remained imprisoned for the rest of their lives. Even their closest family members, unable to reach them in their cage that hung in the sky, eventually forgot about them.

Still climbing and almost out of breath yet within sight

of the corrugated and partly unhinged gates of *Paradise Lost,*
Adamu smiled at Milton's imagination. Literature was not his
strong point. Yet whenever he stumbled upon a crossroad
between a poet's heart and his country's past, he made it a
point to get to the source of it. He knew, for example, that
Milton had found a line in *Genesis* that read:

"From the Garden of Eden flowed four rivers: the
Tigris, the Euphrates, the Pison and the Ghion."

The Ghion, according to the text of the Septuagint
"surrounds the land of Ethiopia."

As one knows since St. Bonaventure, who, together with
Thomas Aquinas, taught in 1255 at the University of Paris,
the Ghion is synonymous with the Nile.

This is how far Adamu got. He could not follow the
great leap Milton took between the actual, earthy spot of the
Garden of Eden and *Amba Geshen.* At this point Adamu,
tired and out of breath, was quite content to trust the blind
poet's intuition.

Apart from his rare visits with the monks on the summit
of cross-shaped *Amba Geshen,* Adamu's only other diversions
were a hunting trip or one of the great Christian holidays.
Then there were the funerals and weddings.

As a young bachelor and officer, he was expected to
attend both occasions in full uniform. He frequently had to
take an uncomfortable mule's ride throughout his district and
sometimes beyond its border. He did not care for either
event. If given a choice, he would have avoided weddings
more than funerals. But his social obligations demanded his
presence under the sometimes large wedding tent or in the
interior of a small, rotund Coptic church.

If he did not enjoy attending marriage ceremonies of
substantial proportions, he hated the small ones of his tenants
even more. Often the bride was still in her early teens. Her
husband was usually much older than she. Most of the time
he was gaunt and brittle like the weatherworn branch of a
tree. Sometimes his waist had taken the balloon shaped
swelling that labels formerly svelte hips and loins with the
price tag of middle age. In many cases the bridegroom was a
widower whose first wife had died after giving birth to more

children than her rawboned body had been capable of.

The marriage was arranged by the bride's parents. The father made the decision while the mother simply listened and the daughter was sent outside her parents' hut. If an agreement was reached, the father of the bride eagerly acknowledged the goats and cows in exchange for one of his scrawny-necked daughters whose future husband had to pay for his wife-to-be. Once purchased, the husband had full possession over his wife. His privileges included beating his spouse whenever he felt like it. Marital rape was so common, it was recognized as the rule rather than the exception.

The bride was usually an undernourished, fine-boned thing accustomed to carrying one of her smaller siblings around wherever she went. Heavily the child sat on her hip during most of the day while she helped her mother. If she was not burdened by a two-year-old brother or sister clinging to her, one saw her with a huge, earthen water jug, unwieldy even without its content. Early in the morning the young girl moved slowly toward a river to get water. A broad leather ribbon was strapped around her perspiring forehead. The throng helped her to carry the jug that was attached to her back and almost broke it as she returned to her mother's hut.

Every day the young girl had to walk two or three miles from her village to the closest river or lake, fill her jug and slowly struggle back home again.

On market days, the big clay pot was replaced with an enormous bundle of fire wood that had to be carried half a day from one village to another, slightly bigger one. Its sale helped to increase the meager income of a voluminous, always hungry family. The young girl was sometimes accompanied by three or four other women. All of them were bent almost double by their far too heavy loads. They were part tree, part Daphne. Their young and pretty faces were contorted from exhaustion. Their small breasts heaved and looked more like quinces than apples. There was no one to relieve their agony. After they had receded a little into the background and had hobbled forward on their bare feet over the hot, dusty road that stretched endlessly toward the mountains, the women, with the wood fastened horizontally across their backs so the width of the branches by far extended the length of their arms, looked like walking crosses.

Two days prior to her wedding day, the bride was usually relieved from any work. Quietly she sat and watched her mother, sisters and other female relatives prepare *injera* and *wott* for the wedding feast. Once or twice during the day she spoke hastily with one of the older women. Insecure and humbly she approached her like a pigeon that feels safer picking its food among its companions rather than by itself.

Apprehensively, the graceful brown-skinned girl gathered strength for her wedding night during which she would be submitted to an ordeal of torture. She was now thirteen years old. At eleven, when she began to menstruate, she had been taken to a special hut where her clitoris had been cut off and thrown outside the door as an unclean, bleeding morsel of flesh to be hastily eaten by a hungry dog. Then, as if this painful and humiliating ordeal had not been enough, she had, under the hands of the wise woman of her tribe, undergone the horrible ritual of infibulation. Both sides of her vagina, considered impure, were pierced with a strong thorn and threaded with a thin strip of leather to hold them together until only the smallest opening was left for her monthly ovulation. Part of the blood whose normal flow was impaired, was held back and caused long lasting cramps each month. All year round there was an awful odor the girl could not get rid of even after bathing in a cold river.

During her wedding night, her husband would take a sharp, dirty knife and cut the leather threads with which she had been sewn together. By now, after two years, leather, hairs and flesh had tightly intermingled. Her skin had grown over the leather like flowers and fruits over a garden fence. The dead skin of an animal had mingled with living nerve endings, muscles and tendons. Her skin, feeding lice, had grown horrible blossoms that would be cut on her wedding night. They would be offered to a ghastly creature luring upon man's mind. In his ignorance and cruel, male vanity, he called this thing that had the wings of Pegasus and the stinking hooves of a hippopotamus, chastity. Its brutal power trampled blindly across dry earth, grass, flowers, herbs and worms. Its heavy feet crushed life and bled the soul.

The drums that played without pausing during the

133

wedding night, announced the approach of the beast. Its arrival was made clear by the shrieks of the bride that again and again pierced through the night and through the eardrums of the wedding guests. But they were used to this inhuman agony and absorbed the fearful cries of the young girl like a lake that swallows flat pebbles flung across its surface by a boy at play. Even the parents of the bride had become insensitive to a ritual that was older than their memories. In the dark corners of their souls they knew that the monster would be killed this night. The bridegroom would destroy it. He would cut into its flesh and drink its blood. He would acknowledge the agony of the dying creature as if it were his own. Its continued cries answered the clamors of his own blood that rushed like a river through his ears and threatened to drown him in his struggle. But the laceration, the sheer physical torment was borne by the young, weak girl alone. It was her blood that flowed through an open wound not the man's. It was she who was needlessly broken and paid an exorbitant price for one of man's most ghastly dreams.

* * *

For five years Adamu had stayed at Geshen. He lived there forgotten by the world. Five years of the prime of his being were spent in total isolation. Life was nothing except one unending day of boredom after another. The days stretched like rope bridges from dawn to dusk across the void of noon. Sometimes he felt as if he lived on the tip of a tongue that belonged to a huge cat whose mouth remained momentarily open, transfixed in a lazy yawn. There was nothing he could do about it. He was under the Emperor's orders.

When, after five years, he was called to Addis Ababa, he considered himself extremely fortunate. He knew his confinement could have been a perpetual one like those of the princes. Once they were imprisoned on top of *Amba Geshen*, most of them never left it. They died there and were quickly put in unmarked graves. Born to be warriors, lovers and kings, they were forced to lead the austere life of monks. With time they could no longer recall what it was like to be free.

Shortly after his arrival in Addis Ababa, Adamu's career took the form of most imperial officers who served the Emperor. It was a demanding and meaningless routine of duty year in and year out, in which personal ambitions were falling stars that for a few seconds illuminated a night sky. His wedding day and the birth of his two children had been such bright sparks.

Looking back upon those celebrations, it seemed to him as if he had unexpectedly entered a deserted ballroom where three luxuriously ornated candelabra with a cluster of candles remained burning even though all other lamps had been extinguished. The smooth glow of the candles with their shadows that created velvety shapes upon the wall softened his heart. His luminous eyes stared into their flames and with an embarrassed sweep of his hand he wiped off a few tear drops that had started to run down his nose.

The coup d'état caught him like a river in flood. Before he knew what was happening, the current had swept him downstream. Once or twice he was held in the deadly embrace of a whirlpool that dragged him under. While he was kept below the surface of the mad river, he felt as if arms were choking him. Before he became unconscious, the image of a seductive woman who clings too tightly to her lover's neck, flashed through his mind. He had almost suffocated before the river spat him up again as if he had been a cherry pit stuck in a boy's throat.

VIII

Wollisso
(Hot springs in Ethiopia)

Adamu Abebe had lived close to a year in exile before he encountered the bachelor's mother. His work at the Emperor's court had gotten him used to European and American women. They were usually the wives of high-ranking foreign officials either in the military or the diplomatic services and he, not being familiar with the countries from which they came, tended to see them as soft, spoiled creatures who seemed to demand a great deal from their husbands and give little in return. Only once in a while did he meet a light skinned woman whose feminine shrewdness did not overshadow her smoothly curved arms and strong white shoulders. Such a female was different from his own women whose slender, honey colored ankles and wrists a man's hand could snap like a twig.

The bachelor's mother looked pleasing enough to him when he first saw her in Wollisso. Sitting close to one side of the pool, he liked to observe her swimming and to see her completely at ease in the water as if she had been born in it. If he squinted his eyes, he had little difficulty in perceiving a fish tail where her legs thrashed the water vigorously. But he was not sure if he enjoyed that.

In spite of her earthy form swimming in the pool straight below him and almost touchable, there was something strange about her. It was as if she were capable of suddenly taking on a shape different from that of a woman. Her limbs that flashed a pinkish-white mixed with silvery streaks, part in the air, part in the water, could suddenly become streamlined and appeared to slither and glide through the liquid substance of the pool without effort. In the midst of broad daylight she sometimes even seemed to be able to disappear altogether as if she had slipped through the bottom of the large, cemented basin. If he blinked his eyes, she vanished and stayed under water for a longer time than lungs were normally capable of.

Yet the moment Adamu left the pool, he forgot her. At night he did not lose any sleep over her. His dreams were filled with his young and lovely wife whom he still missed, not the European woman.

But the next morning, in spite of a slight drizzle, he came back to the pool as if drawn to it against his will. He told himself he needed the exercise and that he had gotten used to his extended, daily swim. Some time ago he discovered that he slept better at night if he kept up swimming on a regular basis. At first, he was just curious to see if the young woman were still there. He thought the rain would discourage her as it usually did with most hotel guests he had seen come and go. The half anticipated sight of her and her two children as he entered the tree enclosed pool area, had a strangely reassuring effect upon him. It brought back short, quick glimpses of several pleasant childhood scenes.

Two or three images came in a fast sequence. They weaved about him in multiple colors, darted from his left to his right side until they formed a complete circle around him. He seemed to float within a miniature rainbow similar to the one caused by a water sprinkler that sprays a parched lawn with its dusty liquid. While he walked along the length of the pool with his eyes fastened upon the woman, he stepped through this shower called forth by his eyes, ears and sense of touch which instantly converted sights and sounds into waking dreams. Like long stemmed flowers in the wind these visions swayed in front of him. They rang the chimes and bells of his imagination and they opened the drawers of his memory where he had stored various tiny toads that carried golden crowns above their protruding eyes. He felt suddenly refreshed and rejuvenated as one experiences it only after a long night of uninterrupted sleep.

With his eyes wide open he seemed to step upon rose-colored gems, sandalwood and blue flowers that resembled violets. For years he had totally forgotten about his hidden treasures across which he now stumbled, slightly hurting his foot on some grass-covered roots of serendipity. Without his being at first aware of it, Adamu felt pulled toward the open, small, soft mouth of the woman whose lips quickly lit up with a sensuous smile. Her look, trying to please, was intuitive like that of an infant who feels the benevolent shadow of Mother falling across its crib. He knew her flashing smile was no more than a reflexive response to her environment.

The young woman who had smiled involuntarily as she saw Adamu approach her, was angry at herself. In the past her smile had often been a reaction to distress and not to joy. Her smile reminded her of the young male baboon she had once observed among a feeding herd gathered under trees. The frightened monkey, bullied by his big leader, used an expression of tenderness as he submitted with loud squeals to the stronger baboon. That image remained with her. Afterwards, even though she knew it was not possible, she wanted her smile to be free of all negative connotations, especially those of cowardice. Being female, she was conditioned by many wombs to a more sensitive and fearful approach toward life than men who were the stronger half of the race. But she valued courage above all other virtues. It was the reason why she admired and envied men and why she imitated them and wanted to be like them. The extra ounces of darkly colored, shriveled flesh that hung between their legs was far less interesting. It was their mental landscape she loved and their greater physical strength. If both traits were richly wrapped and ribboned in one individual, he became irresistible.

Far longer than he intended, Adamu Abebe sat under the lushly growing trees that lined up the length of the Wollisso pool and watched the young woman. He did not know women could swim like this. Most Ethiopian women, never having learned to swim, were frightened by water. It was not so much the athletic abilities the young woman demonstrated that enticed him. He had watched one or two American women swim whose technical skills had been considerably

superior to this young woman's. But it was the childlike joy
which the woman displayed in the shallow and deep ends of
the pool that caught him. Never before had he seen someone
who was so much at home in the water. Every movement of
hers was heavy with pleasure. Like an amphibian, she seemed
to belong more to the sea than the earth. It was her smiling
naiveté that worked upon his heart muscles and loins.

Playing among her children, teasing them by swimming
off into the deep part of the pool where they could not
follow her, she reminded him of a seal who gently, clumsily
shakes off per pups to get herself ready for the hunt. When
she disappeared under water only to emerge again after what
seemed several minutes, there was something uncommon
about her streaming hair and her face. He was sure the bones
around her mouth and eyes had shrunk to childlike
proportions. The water that clung to her skin formed glowing
drops on her face. They looked like pearls mixed with tears.

He remembered fractions of old tales of mermaids and of
Andromeda, the young Ethiopian princess, fastened to her
rock while she waited for the gruesome sea dragon to devour
her.

Losing sight of the young woman as she dove, made him
think she must have trained her lungs and was capable for
brief moments to reverse them again into gills. Those organs
apparently enabled her to bear a lot of weight and to go back
to the *country-under-waves* the poet still sings about but
which is no longer man's home. Adamu felt that the young
woman he could not keep his eyes off, went to a city so dark
and frightening only the blind could find their way. His soul
contracted with despair and disgust. He wanted to leave this
very instant, yet he could not. Awkwardly, as if bound with
ropes, he sat on his chair. His eyes, ears and most of all his
heart were fastened to the woman's mouth and he pressed his
hand against his rib cage to stop its wild fluttering on a
broken wing.

He could not recall how long he remained seated. As one
of the woman's shoulders lifted above the glittering surface
only to disappear again within a split second, she reminded
him of someone whose presence he once had felt as if he had
eyes on the back of his head. Yet when he turned around the
woman had broken away. She had dissolved into the earth

again from where she had momentarily risen with the smell of the dead still clinging to her gray clothes. Her small, ashen face, the clumsy, helpless movement of her foot had torn his heart.

The young woman was not sure what to think of the Ethiopian and his rude stares she instantly forgave. With his large eyes and full lips that were unhindered by a mustache she found him desirable. Across his symmetrical features, straight-nosed like those she had seen on an ancient Greek coin, sadness spread in wild, unruly lines like scars. It was not the distress of a woman who covers her face with the perfumed veils of Salome. This man's grief was a savage one that had eaten part of his face. Like an earthworm it had crawled across his forehead and had crisscrossed it until it reached the roots of his hair. It had taken chunks of flesh out of his face and replaced it with something that was more than skin, muscles and small facial bones. Slowly, over many years, sadness had vertically descended upon his face until it reached his lower lip which it gripped with pliers and bent both of its corners downward. Brutally life had pawed his face. Out of his one face, it had created a succession of faces that walked down the steps of ancestry.

Now, while even his smile was a little sad, his face covered the abyss of time. There was music under his brown skin and she could hear the doleful cry of a pelican that sits in front of the unreachable splendor of a horizon. Slowly, the bird was floating on top of small, dark-gray water snakes and the ugliness of man. Adamu's face had the closed mouth of Rilke's god and of a black marble statue partly buried in sand. Around it, the sea weaved her salt and songs. And as she looked again at him, she thought his was a face that would not grow old.

The young woman's children took their afternoon nap usually about 1:00 p.m. right after they had lunch in the almost empty dining room where the barefooted waiters had yawned openly. Even away from home and his accustomed bed, her son fell asleep within minutes of having been gently rocked by Almas. Her daughter was a different matter. Smaller, more vulnerable but fighting sleep fiercely, she was far more restless and sometimes wriggled for close to half an hour in Almas's arms while the nanny paced endlessly up and

140

down the room. The patience of the little nursemaid seemed limitless and the young woman admired her for it. When both children slept and the entire hotel seemed to take a nap, their mother often brought a pillow and placed it next to the steps of her miniature sunken pool in the bathroom, a chip of the large, outdoor pool. Peacefully she rested there next to the steaming water. Her vigorous swims during the mornings had made her pleasantly tired and she often also fell asleep in the stillness of noon.

She always dreamt. Small, unconnected pieces of her mind swirled and floated through her subterranean caves. Most of her dreams were not worth remembering. In trying to sort them out she felt like one of the cleaning women in her husband's office who rummage^S at night through a wastepaper basket to look for a discarded magazine or newspaper. But some dreams had significance. They were like a phone call one receives unexpectedly from forgotten friends who live thousands of miles away. Those dreams were transparent baubles of various size and shape, that brought back a lost piece of the past. These reveries were miniature islands that had broken away from the mainland and now drifted forlornly on their own. Their messages, if one could decipher their meaning, were important. They contained the past, present and future all rolled up in one lump like that huge transparent plastic ball she had on one occasion watched the wind blow across the surface of the sea.

* * *

After her first encounter with Adamu, the young woman had a nightmare. As she slept, her body lay motionlessly at the edge of the pool. One sharp, careless movement toward the wrong side would have inundated her. While sleeping, her eyelashes formed the same sickle-shaped half circle of the moon as those of her children in the other, darker room that was rendered still by drawn curtains. As her eyelids were slightly raised and lowered by the fast moving pupils underneath, her soul walked in shallow, marshy waters that reeked with oil and filth.

Railway tracks ran along a marshland out of which a bloodred sun swam slowly. As far as one could see, the

141

surface of the water was only interrupted by dead wood which partly floated and was partly anchored in brown-black mud. Here and there the silver dots of sea gulls formed a bridalwreath on the brow of an enormous wasteland.

Then the dreamer saw an old woman who was tied to the tracks and she heard a black-skinned man, dressed in a business suit, say he would kill his captive. Someone ran for help and came to a highway that was built alongside a small town. The racing figure, whom the dreamer could only see from the back, was clothed in a long, gray skirt. Its seam that was heavy and wet, trailed along the ground unless it was held up by one hand. Then the figure made a left turn where the highway began its descent down a long hill.

After a while the figure tried to stop a car. Yet as soon as she held up a hand, all cars came to a halt as if they obeyed a red traffic light. The figure remembered the tied-up woman and became terrified. At that instant, before she could take another step, the cars started to move again. Every car the figure tried to stop was driven by a black man. The figure was afraid and did not want to get into the car.

Suddenly, the figure realized she had no make-up on and that her hair was loosened. She tried to find a ladies room. While she put on lipstick, the figure became aware that she lost precious time and that the old woman might be killed before she could get back with help. But even though the figure felt guilty in wasting time by beautifying herself, she continued to do so. All her movements were in slow motion.

Finally, the figure got back to the highway. She now accepted a ride from a black man. He was an elderly person and kind. Her anxiety vanished but she was apprehensive about lost time. When they got back to the tracks, the old woman had been killed. Pieces of her body still clung to the tracks. Yet her head and most of her left hip had been carried away by the train. Children, as small as mice, scurried back and forth over the remains of the body.

The bachelor's mother screamed and woke up. In the darkened room the stillness around her was only interrupted by a faint gurgle from the pool. It was the knowledge that her children continued to sleep which eventually calmed her down enough to get up and put on her dress. As she buttoned it in the back, she noticed her fingers were shaking.

* * *

When the young woman left the hotel room, she remembered a train trip she had taken not too long ago from Addis Ababa to Dire Dawa. The small, pleasant town whose streets were lined with fig trees in full bloom, is situated halfway to Djibouti, the unbearably hot and sandy capital of French Somaliland.

Her husband, her small son and herself had spent about twelve hours on the train that made only one scheduled stop at Auwash. The station was a gateway between the mountainous highlands with its cool air full of shadows and cliffs and the desert where vertical shapes and shade were rare.

The moment the train had rested next to a wooden platform, the lower part of its windows were embellished with mango and papaya carrying young women who walked below the passenger's heads. Gracefully, with low pleading voices, the women offered the fruits they either carried on their heads, or when getting ready for a sale, under bare breasts.

The railway gate led to a large stretch of flat, sun-eaten land, sweltering with heat and empty of people but with miles of single acacia trees and bushes in clusters here and there that had grown unperturbed for centuries. It was shortly before the rainy season and the ground had opened every few feet, exposing the parched earth like the cuts of a finger.

The young woman, who a moment ago had talked with her husband as the burned earth rushed by, became silent and sad when she saw how torn the country was. After about three hours of a slow, sweltering train ride that rocked its passengers into drowsiness, the landscape got interrupted by rivers and hot springs. As if by magic, the ground turned into luscious, wild, wet gardens where small alligators swam around cows hooves and their lean legs that stood knee deep in bubbling water.

"How come the gators do not attack the cattle?" she asked naively her husband.

143

"They have enough to eat. They are not hungry, just playful," he had answered.

Several more hours passed slowly while most passengers sat on wooden benches with their heads nodding and their bodies drooping from the heat. Then without warning, the train suddenly came to a full halt. A child, caught unaware, fell off its seat and started to cry. As everybody quickly discovered, there was no particular reason for their stop except that in spite of blowing constantly a whistle, the engineer had run over a cow caught on the tracks. The train did not have a cattle guard and had severed most of the animal's limbs before it had finally killed it. The engine had dragged the rest of the hapless bovine with it before it was able to slow down. It was a horrible sight. The young woman made sure her son did not get a glimpse of it.

As soon as the engineer stepped off the train, a fierce, verbal battle ensued between him and the owner of the cow as well as about thirty villagers who had run from their *tukuls* when they heard the train stop. In the midst of shouts and screams from the angry peasants some of whom swung sticks and knives at the engineer and passengers alike, the remains of the cow had to be pulled out from under the train. Before it could move again, the engineer had to pacify the peasants who wanted to be recompensed for the loss of the cow. For the village people the animal constituted a highly prized possession.

As soon as the young woman recollected the train trip, she found relief in making a connection between the slain cow and her awful dream. Part of her dream and the train trip seemed to have merged into one event.

* * *

Three days after the bachelor's mother had first seen Adamu Abebe, she felt disturbed and irritated for no particular reason. In the evening she sat as usual by herself at her table in the dining room of the hotel. Even though it was only about 8:00 p.m., night had dropped like a stage curtain about two hours ago and lay heavily outside the rain-bathed windows.

She felt bored beyond words. The few hotel guests who

144

were present did not interest her. Rather embarrassed she had turned down an invitation to gamble. Before dinner, while Almas put the children to bed, she spoke briefly with her husband. He had arranged to pick them up the following day. "Are you glad to get back home?" he asked her. "Yes," she lied knowing that he would not accept any other answer. Even after the waiter had cleared the table she remained in her chair. As her finger circled the rim of her water glass, she went over every word her husband had said. She knew his voice well and was able to detect the slightest nuance in it. She was relieved to discover that he sounded normal. He seemed happy to get her and the children back. She sighed and looked about her.

The hotel was the only attempt at civilization for many miles around. Except for a well-stocked bar that held no attraction for her, there was no entertainment.

The young woman felt as if she were caught in a net. Boredom stuck to her like the spit of a spider. With wide open eyes yet dreaming she saw a net. It was the great hair net of the horned moon she drags slowly through the ocean. The net holds everyone and dreadful harm comes to all creatures who slip between its holes. They fall forever through bottomless space where the fierce Maenads live next to maelstroms.

The hotel was like the center of a small shell contained within the big net. From the isolated building many trails ran invisibly into the night. Like a red, ripe August moon the pathways formed a perfect circle. No one was able to travel upon those routes except the spider whose hidden presence and murderous intent the young woman sensed with every vein of her body. She shuddered and felt suddenly cold. There was no one in the quiet room to whom she could turn. For a while she sat motionless. No visible sign of life about her struck the eye. She could have been a statue. Cold and lifeless.

Then she felt something walking inside her. It was someone who stumbled across stones and rocks and she saw a desert where life was reduced to its roots, and where the wind drew dusty circles upon mounds of sand. There was no sound except for a whisper. Even though she cocked her ear, strained nerves and muscles and tried to turn herself into an

145

ear, she could not understand what the voice had to say. She knew the message was important. But it was as if someone had shouted from a mountain top or as if a voice had sung on another star and then died. By the time the voice reached her ear that now stood upright upon desert sand, it was reduced to an inaudible shade. Within the murmur she heard the rustling of a full skirt and the faintest sound of water, as if someone had forgotten to turn off a kitchen faucet. Her tongue licked off the tears that ran along her nose and she thought a swim in the warm water of the pool would distract her mind.

* * *

She thought she knew Wollisso's pool well from her many swims. But that night it looked different. It suddenly seemed larger and much farther away from the hotel. Its outlines were not clearly defined. There were no lights except glimmers from a fast moving moon. Hotel guests were not encouraged to bathe after it got dark. The water lay black and motionless in front of her. Silent and taller than during the day, the trees loomed above the water. The odor of mimosa was so strong that her head started to spin slightly. She swallowed greedily large mouthfuls of the intoxicating scent. Tree frogs tapped their rhythmic songs upon the back of the night. She quickly slipped out of her clothes and dove into the pool. Silkily, like a hand she liked, the warm water caressed her skin.

It took her less than a second to realize two things. She was not alone in the water and the pool was not the one she knew. Then she thought happily, "Well, I have always wanted to swim in the Ligurian sea, the one out of which Carrara rose, the marble mountain." She smiled and remembered that from this quarry Michaelangelo had given birth to his David, his Moses and his young, fragile Mary who holds an angelic, nude Christ on her lap—a lover rather than a son. Shyly she has sat for the past four hundred years in a corner of the world's largest cathedral. Her dead eyes are hungry with unfulfilled love.

The young woman had imagined that the waters of the Ligurian sea, normally emerald green with a yellowish hue and white crowns, would turn into a velvety charcoal at night. This was not so. In certain places she noticed that the small, choppy waves were filled with powdery drops of light, prisms of diamonds. Like will-o'-the-wisps they interrupted the black blanket of the water. There were enough of them to let her easily submerge and glide in and out between imaginary edifices. And once more she recognized Debussy's cathedral and water covered rocks.

Under the sea's surface the silence was, as always, almost complete. Its only interruption were faint echoes filtering through the darkness. They were caused by underwater currents nearby. But she thought they came from breakers at the shore whose ceaseless rustle back and forth was the sea's breath. The sea inhaled and exhaled with a rhythmic movement that has not been interrupted for these past million years. And she knew as long as the sea breathed like this, there would be life.

All at once she felt surrounded by smaller and larger fish, sometimes including one with a triangular fin. They eyed her without curiosity. A moray passed her within inches. Its slithery, sickly white body cut the water in elegant arabesques. More snake than eel, the muraena glided next to her without trying to bite her. Within a few seconds it disappeared under a crevice. The young woman seemed a familiar shape to these eels and fish.

She had always wanted to dive deeply. Now she felt a little sleepy from having sat at the shore where she had sung her usual songs, carefully timing her voice to the rhythm of the breakers. Then, without blinking her eyes, she was way below the surface. A thousand tons of water weighed weightlessly above her.

Her goal tonight was an overhanging cliff. Its rough edges were covered with corals. She recalled that she had always wanted to explore the cave which lay underneath the reef. Apparently it was the abode of some larger fish. The creaks of the cliff were caused by a gently swaying, huge mass of freely floating, only loosely connected corals and seaweeds. The eerie noise frightened her. She had seen large pieces of rock suddenly and silently fall off. They crushed fish and other sea creatures beneath them. While tumbling, they had turned the dark waters an ugly, greasy gray. If she were caught among the crashing debris, its pounding and grinding force would reduce her into shreds. Her present shape would no longer be recognizable.

But tonight, she had to take the risk. She had long thought about swimming to this cave. For a while now her entire existence had circled endlessly around the same goal. The moment her mind wandered freely, it returned to the grotto. She dreamt about it while she slept on the sea's surface. The moment she woke up, the cave's vision and its unidentified content was in front of her eyes. Only when she was entirely absorbed hunting fish, found her soul temporary relief from the cave's persistent pursuit.

The rocks groaned while she quickly passed them. But they held, nothing broke off. Even her skin remained unscratched. The cave was smaller than she thought. Not much bigger than a large room. Some dark forms were dimly contoured. As far as she could make out, they were small coral beds that clustered near the rocky bottom. Their branches filled several niches and crevices. There was plenty of uninterrupted space the moment she swam a little higher. She lightly touched rough walls which rose straight up. For a while she glided back and forth under what seemed to be the roof of the cavern. Its surface was hard when she approached it.

Before long she noticed that on top of a larger growth of corals rested living matter. Whether fish or other sea creature, it was as aware of her presence as she was of his. The animated substance did not move. At rest, it seemed to invite her to come closer. She slowly started to circle it. Then, encouraged by its apparent gentleness, she lightly touched it. It only took one strong movement and she was out of its reach. Excitedly, she swam back and forth, moving close to the roof of the cave. Finally, getting curious again, she approached once more this softly breathing and calm living being.

This time she had come too close. What seemed to be two strong arms clasped her around mid-waist and held her close to its own body. Its grip was firm but did not hurt. Her fears subsided quickly. Her heart started to beat normally again. If this living thing harmed her now, she would no longer be able to defend herself. She could no longer run away.

The young woman had come to this cave of her own will. She had hoped it would contain some forbidden treasure she wanted to investigate. Now she had passed the threatening rocks without being crushed by them. Not having come to harm by entering the grotto, she was not sure how she would exit it again. Or even if she were leaving it at all. Whatever happened from now on was no longer under her control. Something much stronger and bigger than herself surrounded her. Its presence filled the entire subterranean area. It went outside of it, way into the sea where instead of diminishing, it still continued. It was like a huge river that for quite a while holds its own sweet water against the bitter one of the sea.

These thoughts ran dimly in the back of her mind that seemed to have slipped to the lower end of her body. All she was aware of from now on was a smooth strength mixed with gentleness and agility. It was as if most of her had turned into skin and sensations. She had become a streamlined shape of flesh and muscles. She barely sensed that the tendons, spine and bones she clung to comprised a complicated being. The other form that held her seemed to be part of her own flesh. But its flashes and sparks of thoughts flickered like blue flames only within its own skull. Those were totally out of her reach. Skin could be touched, bones could be held but feelings could not.

She had lost her voice. The only sounds were two breaths, staccato, like runners who had come from far. Mouth met mouth. Tongues interwove and explored slippery, steep surfaces of enamel. The sense of taste was acute. It gradually became more and more stimulated by fresh and healthy odors. They led to further movements, and to more intense sensations that inflamed the taste buds and strongly mixed with the sense of touch.

To increase their pleasure they moved briefly away from each other and for sheer joy glided along the walls of the cave. With one quick stroke they pushed themselves up toward its roof, then descended again effortlessly. They constantly changed their positions. Soon, they both swam along the interior of the cave. They were only barely aware of its craggy outlines and almost did not notice the rocks outside the cave that continued their creaky, ghostly song.

Never had she played such a game before. Sometimes she was imagining it could be like this. Earlier, when it had come to an actual encounter between a potential lover and herself, she mostly withdrew. Trying to get rid of her love stricken pursuer, she appeared from a distance to be an inviting landscape where shade and sunny places lured a lost wanderer to rest. But as soon as he approached, she changed into a clam-like substance. And if the stroller came too close, she swiftly withdrew behind protective walls. He, who had been beckoned by a sparkling shape whose contours were embellished by his own mind, saw just one eye viewing him with hostility between two calcified barriers. So narrow were they, nothing except the gentle touch of a hand, could pass. Even that risked getting caught and becoming transfixed to one spot. When actual invasion did occur, just like Napoleon's army did enter Moscow, she had fled from a burning city. Somewhere in a small village of Russia's endless steppes, she lay hidden until the enemy left. He, who was but a frustrated victor trying to go home, his life threatened by icy winds and frozen rivers. Between Moscow and Paris *la Grande Armée* perished. And Tchaikovsky made fun of *la Marseillaise*.

This night she wanted to take a calculated risk. She had changed into something she did not know she could be. Her sense of smell and taste became intoxicated. Water and air seemed to be filled with wine. She became a little reckless. Feelings of guilt and shame that had hunted her so often, slowly dissolved. Astonished, she realized that this was a game played according to fixed rules. It was not, as her romantic phantasies had imagined, a matter of life and death. Even though her opponent was more forceful than herself, she did not need to be afraid of him. This was not a medieval joust where one knight by stamina, skill or luck might kill the other. It was a more gentle contest. By the same token the stakes were higher than simply winning or losing.

* * *

When the young woman woke up the next morning, it took her several seconds to realize where she was. For a long moment she still seemed to float on the surface of the sea instead of lying on the narrow hotel bed she had finally gotten used to. With her hair all dry, her swim the night before now seemed like a dream. But still strongly caught by it, she moved far slower than normally and almost was not ready when her husband came to pick them up.

As they were getting ready for lunch and their immediate return to Addis Ababa afterward, with the children taking their nap in the car, there was a commotion outside the back entrance of the hotel. Visible from where husband and wife stood and past the wide open glass doors of the dining room, was a steep, short hill. Densely growing plants and trees were interrupted by several narrow footpaths. The abundant vegetation gave shelter to a few cabins that were sprinkled like oversized mushrooms across the compound. These additional hotel accommodations were preferred by guests who wanted more privacy and were not afraid of wild dogs and hyenas, the nightly visitors who prowled around the isolated, round buildings protected by a straw roof. Unlike the noisy tin roofs, the straw covered huts softened the hard rains to a large extent.

Out of the hill and its high, winding trails the voices seemed to come. The more the small family listened, the more they distinguished some women wailing like those cries performed by professional mourners. One or two male voices mingled lowly with the women's shrill ones until they seemed to be right under their windows. Yet, when the young woman and her husband walked toward the dining room, all sounds had subsided to murmurs and there was nothing unusual about the small, sleepy crowd who had gathered for lunch.

It was only after they had put their belongings into the car and started to drive out of the hotel's tree-lined property that they saw a group of Ethiopian women next to the road. They wore torn, black dresses. Their terrible chant, the rocking motion of their necks and breasts while they squatted on the ground with their knees spread wide apart as if ready to give birth, made husband and wife stop their car and inquire who died. When the bachelor's father, who spoke Galla in addition to Amharic, turned around to face his wife, he made a helpless shrug with his left shoulder before he started the engine again.

She had never become used to this insignificant gesture

of his that had upset her many times. Part of its helplessness signaled pure annoyance. Another portion of his defenselessness was born out of a submission to her desires that were alien to his own. His shrug was like the offering of flowers with a contemptuous glance. His first impulse, a good one, was counterbalanced by a rational reflection that threw its shadow across soft red petals. It showed her that emotionally he was still caught in the wetlands of infantile compulsions and had only one foot on the shore of reason, the gift, hard won, of a mature man. Her husband's vacillation between two countries, the one of the child and the one of the adult, each still strongly conflicting with each other and each expressing itself in a different language, made her waver as well.

Her own world was also unstable. She too, even though perhaps less than he, constantly still lived partly as a child and partly as a woman. Half of her was forgetting one language and half was acquiring a new one, and she expressed herself adequately in neither. Her doubts were so numerous that they often broke her down. It was as if a writing desk carried too many paper weights. The desk was solid and perfectly capable of supporting any amount of heavy loads of paper. In her insecurity though, she saw the entire surface of the desk covered with nothing but highly polished brass paper weights. Thousands of them. Their shiny surface made her feel as if the legs of the desk were going to break and pull her down. Through the floor of the ceiling and through other floors below her she saw herself sinking fifty floors deep until she could move no further and debris cut off her breath. It was a ludicrous and frightening perception that clung to her as if glued upon her soul.

Repeatedly during their six years of marriage when the young woman had looked upon her husband, she knew she had wed a prince who changed into a frog after she had kissed him. Before they had gotten married, he was more appealing than any other man she had up to then watched from under semi-closed eyelids. But once he wore a wedding ring, he changed. Never daring to look fully, she saw her husband revert slowly to an amphibian when during their loveplay their limbs intertwined. His legs, stronger and more enduring than hers, pulled her into his kingdom built from mud and slime. Once within his power, he voluptuously suffocated her amidst shells and pearls.

Immense and totally foreign were his culture and his people. His race sang in tongues she could not accept. Kindly, his women tried to teach her. But with stubbornness and pride steeped in fear that made her rigid like a wooden board, she refused to learn. Raised for twenty years in the most terrible, the most cruel and the most helpless of all Germanies, the young woman was unable and unwilling to become an Armenian. She did not want to adopt to a language so refined and so ancient that it sounded barbarian again. The snake had bitten into its own tail. Her Germanic traits, innate and learned ones, had been whipped under her skin. Now she was incapable of discarding them, unless, snake-like she were able to throw off her skin. She was not happy while she was brought up in Germany and while love for her country was fed to her with every smile and sun ray that caressed mountains and rivers. She understood that her hate and shame and fear of all things German were inseparably interwoven within that great love. And there were times when she had feverently wished not to be German. Yet once she started to live beyond the limits of the soil that had borne her, she became fiercely German.

* * *

The ride from Wollisso to Addis Ababa took several hours. As they drove along a highway where for miles their car was the only one on the road, the young woman's husband's shrug was accompanied by a mumbled sentence.

"They found a dead Ethiopian in the pool. He was most probably too drunk and fell in . . . these people! They do not even know how to swim."

Contemptuously, and suddenly aware that he was an inadequate swimmer himself who was afraid of water, he started to drive faster. His eyes concentrated upon the road that was more used by donkeys, heavy bellied mules, the small, sturdy Galla horses and swiftly walking, white-dressed Ethiopians, than by cars or trucks.

He did not see how his wife's face became small and how it shrank and turned ashen. Only when she started to retch, did he pay attention to her. He had hardly time to pull the car over to the side of the road, before she vomited her lunch.

"What is the matter with you? Are you not feeling well?" he wanted to know.

"I am fine. There must have been something in the food," she managed to say and smiled faintly at him. As he started the car once more, she leaned her head against the back of the seat and closed her eyes.

On the long way home the bachelor's father observed his wife's face several times while she slumbered next to him. He thought she did not look as well as he had expected her to after her vacation. She was too pale. Used to his own women's skin of a darker pigment, he above all had coveted her fair face. It reminded him of a white sea-bird. Later, after he had gotten to know her during their marriage, it was not so much her soft whiteness that pulled him toward her, but a frailty in the middle of her round face that was so much like the moon. There was something gray and bloodless that seemed to hover above and below her high cheek bones. It was at once infantile and very old. It often elicited his vigor and his maleness.

Then taking him by surprise, she was like a bird capable of flying off on her own wings and leaving him behind, bound to a rock. She mocked him from above. And he hated her intensely at those moments. Or like a mad bird she suddenly charged at him and pecked him so he became terrified she would blind him. Then, just as unexpectedly, she could be sweet and gentle, her voice competing with that of a thrush. There could be a balminess about her, as vast and as dark as the ocean across which she was able to fly. It was the same ocean that one night during a storm, would pull her down, pluck her white feathers out of the sky and bury them amidst the crest of the waves.

The bachelor's father, as he watched his wife's face across which sleep had softly drawn a transparent veil, started to feel ill. He loved his wife, yet his love was immature and possessive. He clung to her like an infant in fear of losing its mother. There was an insatiable thirst for her in him that could not be quenched, no matter how many times he made love to her. He had come to know the woman he slept with night after night. Hundreds of nights. They all seemed alike. Now, when he looked back, those nights were like a row of pearls. He no longer remembered that each pearl had grown in her own shell and in her own bed of mud. Every night had been different, but from a distance they looked the same. Their similarity blurred his vision. He grew more nauseated.

He thought he knew his wife. He thought he understood the mother of his two children whose body he had explored to the fullest. Had he not, like Ahab, stood night after night on the deck of his ship? Had he not put his foot on her neck and made her his slave? Had he not conquered all women by overpowering this one? He knew every curve of her and every hue of her skin was familiar to him. Like Ahab though, he also knew he sailed only the surface of the sea. He never went below it. He was cowed by the monster that lurked in the depth. Afraid, he craved it with all his heart. More than anything he wanted to obtain and destroy it.

Every so often, particularly during moonlit nights, he saw it rise and he hated its huge contours. With all his power and maleness he pursued it. Nothing did he loathe more, nothing did he want to kill more than this enormous, elusive mass surrounding his wife. It was like a shadow which seemed to loom constantly beyond the deck of the ship. It swam about her, frolicked among the waves, mocked him who clung to a few wooden boards between sea and sky. Sometimes the white form seemed to become one with the water and the horizon. If the elusive shape appeared during the day which was rare, it usually was covered by a mist. And the vapor could grow as thick as a London fog. He invariably got lost in it. Helpless like a child he then stirred his solid ship until he grew mad and stabbed at the unknown body. Under the fog he cold hear it breathe but he could not see it. It seemed to turn his heart into a stone and it contracted his lungs so he almost fainted.

During the worst nights he became desperate and took a small boat with only four crew members. For hours they rowed without seeing anything. But they keenly felt the monster's presence. Blindly, filled with fear and seething rage, he struck again and again. Yet there was only air. He grew angrier and angrier, started to move about, rock the unsteady boat and wildly swung his harpoon. The four sailors who were with him, saw that he had become insane. Yet there was nothing they could do. Nobody except Ahab had ever seen the evasive silhouette.

Then one night suddenly he hit something solid. His harpoon crashed into a creature. It was hard as if made of glass and steel. His weapon was struck out of his hand. Then came a second impact, much harder. This time he received a tremendous blow. It felt as if a large knife penetrated his brain between nose and forehead. He fell unconscious.

When he awoke again, his wife slumbered innocently next to him. Her face was that of a babe. Yet she had changed. He no longer knew her. He groaned with pain.

"I am going to kill you," he cried through clenched teeth. His wife looked at him. Her eyes were wide and black with fear.

"Are you crazy?" she whispered.

Then floating past her, as if carried on an invisible stretcher, she saw the face and body of Adamu Abebe. His hands were neatly folded under his chest. A long gray gown covered him from the neck to his feet. Just his brown toes, perfectly shaped as only those are whose feet had walked barefoot through most of childhood and adolescence, were visible at the seam of his shroud.

* * *

It was the end of October now. The crisp mornings required the first heat in the house to warm finger tips and toes where the circulation no longer worked as well. Outside the bachelor's closed windows, from where the green summer screens had been removed, the light was clear. It was of such a translucent gold that it awoke cravings in him to take long walks in the woods that were ablaze in fall colors. To be free, he thought. The sky was one magnificent sheet of blue. It made him forget how black the horizon was just beyond the sun's reach. It was the blackness of space into which the astronauts had dipped their wings. The golden blueness made him feel like a prisoner behind invisible bars. He became aware of a wasp flying sluggishly in the window. Its humming no longer sounded fierce and angry as it had during the hot summer months.

"I have to kill it," he thought and then quickly forgot about it. This morning he found the wasp dead on his polished wooden floor. It was a tiny spot of black dust. He could barely see its yellow stripes, its proud insignia, any longer.

About the Author

Born and raised in Germany, Ursula Wilfriede Schneider has a Ph.D. in Comparative Literature concentrating in German and French from the Graduate School, City University of New York. She has taught at Hunter College in New York and Montclair State University in New Jersey. She writes short stories, travelogues and novels. She has two children.